Double Act

Double Act

RUBY
illustrated
by
Nick Sharratt

GARNET
illustrated
by
Sue Heap

JACQUELINE WILSON

DELACORTE PRESS

Published by
Delacorte Press
Bantam Doubleday Dell Publishing Group, Inc.
1540 Broadway
New York, New York 10036

Copyright © 1995 by Jacqueline Wilson
Inside illustrations © Nick Sharratt (Ruby) and Sue Heap (Garnet)
By arrangement with Transworld Publishers Ltd.
First American edition 1998
Originally published in the UK by Doubleday, 1995

The trademark Delacorte Press® is registered in the U.S. Patent and Trademark Office and in other countries.

Library of Congress Cataloging-in-Publication Data

Wilson, Jacqueline.
   Double act / Jacqueline Wilson ; illustrated by Nick Sharratt
[and] Sue Heap.—1st American ed.
      p.   cm.
   "Ruby illustrated by Nick Sharratt, Garnet illustrated by Sue Heap."
   Summary: Ten-year-old twins Ruby and Garnet try to deal with the big
changes in their lives when their father starts dating and they face the pos-
sibility of being separated.
   ISBN 0-385-32312-3
   [1. Twins—Fiction.   2. Sisters—Fiction.   3. Single-parent family—
Fiction.   4. Individuality—Fiction.]   I. Sharratt, Nick, ill.   II. Heap,
Sue, ill.   III. Title.
PZ7.W6957Do   1998
[Fic]—dc21   97-8744
                                                                        CIP
                                                                         AC

The text of this book is set in 12.5-point New Aster.
Book design by Julie E. Baker

Manufactured in the United States of America
March 1998
10 9 8 7 6 5 4 3 2 1
BVG

For Anne, Derek, Thorne, and Franca Dorothy

We're twins. I'm Ruby. She's Garnet.

We're identical. There's very few people who can tell us apart. Well, until we start talking. I tend to go on and on. Garnet is much quieter.

That's because I can't get a word in edgeways.

1

We are exactly the same height and weight. I eat a bit more than Garnet. I love candy, and I like salty things too. I once ate thirteen bags of potato chips in one day. All salt-and-vinegar flavor. I love lots of salt and vinegar on french fries too. French-fried potatoes are my special weakness. I go munch munch munch gulp and they're gone. So then I have to scarf some of Garnet's. She doesn't mind.

Yes I do.

I don't get fatter because I run around more. I hate sitting still. Garnet will sit hunched over a book for hours, but I get the fidgets. We're both good at running, Garnet and me. At our last intramural sports day at school we beat everyone, even the boys. We came in first. Well, I did, actually. Garnet came in second. But that's not surprising, seeing that I'm the oldest. We're both ten. But I'm twenty minutes older. I was the bossy baby who pushed out first. Garnet came second.

We live with our dad and our grandmother.

Dad often can't tell us apart in the morning at breakfast, but then his eyes aren't always quite open. He just swallows black coffee as he jumps into his clothes and then dashes off for his train. Dad works in an office in London and he hates it. He's always tired out when he gets home. But he can tell us apart by then. It's easier in the evening. My braids are generally coming undone and my T-shirt's probably stained. Garnet stays as neat as a pin.

That's what our grandmother says. Gran always used to have pins stuck all down the front of her cardigan. We had to be very careful when we hugged her. Sometimes she even had pins sticking out of her mouth. That was when she did her dressmaking. She used to work in this exclusive boutique, pinning and tucking and sewing all day long. Then, after . . .

Well, Gran had to look after us, you see, so she did dressmaking at home. For private customers. Mostly very large ladies who wanted the latest fashions. Garnet and I always got the giggles when we peeped at them in their underwear.

Gran made all our clothes too. That was *awful*. It was bad enough Gran being old-fashioned and making us have our hair in braids. But our clothes made us a laughingstock at school, though some of the mothers said we looked a perfect picture.

We had frilly dresses in summer and dinky pleated skirts in winter, and Gran knitted too— angora boleros that made us itch, and matching sweaters and cardigans for the cold. Twinsets. And a very silly set of twins we looked too.

But then Gran's arthritis got worse. She'd always had funny fingers and a bad hip and a trick knee. But soon she got so she'd screw up her face when she got up or sat down, and her fingers swelled sideways and she couldn't make them work.

She can't do her dressmaking now. It's a shame, because she loved doing it so much. But there's one Amazing Advantage. We get to wear store-bought clothes now. And because Gran can't really make it on the bus into town, we get to *choose*.

Well . . . Ruby gets to choose.

I choose for both of us. T-shirts. Tights. Jeans. Matching ones, of course. We still want to look alike. We just want to look normal.

Only I suppose we're not really like the normal sort of family you read about in books. We read a lot of books. Dad is the worst. He keeps on and on buying them—not just new ones, but heaps of old dusty tomes from book sales and auctions and thrift shops. We've run out of shelves. We've even run out of floor. We've got piles and piles of books in every room and you have to zigzag around them carefully or you cause a bookquake. If you have ever been attacked by fifty or a hundred very hard hardbacks then you'll know this is to be avoided at all costs. There are big boxes of books upstairs too that Dad hasn't gone through yet. Sometimes you have to climb clear over them to get somewhere vital like the toilet.

Gran keeps moaning that the floorboards won't stand up to all that weight. They do tend to creak a bit. Dad gets flustered then and agrees it's ridiculous, and sometimes when we're a bit hard up for cash he loads a few boxes into our old car and takes them to a secondhand bookshop to sell. He does sell them too—but he nearly always comes back with another load of bargains, books he couldn't possibly resist.

Then Gran goes at him again and Dad gets all moody, but when he brings her a big sack of blockbuster romances from a flea market she softens up considerably. Gran likes to sit in her special chair with lots of plumped-up cushions at her back, her little legs propped up on her footstool, a box of chocolates wedged in beside her, and a juicy love story in her lap. They're sometimes very sexy, and when Garnet and I read over her shoulder she swats us away, saying we'll find out something we shouldn't. Ho ho. We found it all out *ages* ago.

Dad reads large fat books too, but they're not modern, they're all classics—Charles Dickens and Thomas Hardy. If we have a look at Dad's book we wonder what the Dickens they're about and they seem *very* Hardy, but Dad likes them. He also likes boys' adventure books—really old ones where the boys wear knickers and talk like twits: "I say, old bean," and "Truly spiffing," and "Tophole."

Garnet likes old books too—stuff like *Little Women* and *What Katy Did* and all those E. Nesbit books. And she reads twin books too. Books like *The Twins at St. Clare's*. And all the *Sweet Valley Twins*. I read them too, because you can read them nice and quickly. But the books *I* like best are true stories about flashy famous people. Actors and actresses. I skip everything boring and just read the best parts when they're on TV and making movies and all over the front of the newspapers, very flashy and very famous.

We're going to be famous too someday, you bet. So I've started writing our life story already. It's funny, Garnet is usually the one who writes stuff. Her writing's neater than mine. So often I get her to do my homework. She doesn't mind.

Yes I do.

I was going through one of the boxes of books upstairs and right at the bottom there was this lovely fat red book. Ruby red, with a leather spine and one word picked out in gold lettering: ACCOUNTS.

I thought it was the title but when I opened it up there were just all these blank pages.

I asked Dad what had happened to the story and he said it wasn't a real book at all. Accounts are addition. You add up everything you've bought. That's keeping accounts.

"Only I don't like keeping accounts. I just feel guilty seeing how much I've spent," said Dad. "You can have it to scribble in, twins."

So I'm scribbling away.

I'm not.

Yes you are. I keep letting you have a turn. And I'm not just writing about me, I'm writing about us. Giving an account of ourselves. Hey, Garnet, find a dictionary and look up the word *account.*

Account: 1. A verbal or written report, description, or narration of some occurrence, event, etcetera.

Yeah! That's exactly what I'm doing. Writing an account of our lives.

Everything's a bit boring right this minute but maybe soon we'll somehow get our big chance and we'll achieve our lifetime's ambition and be actresses.

I don't want to be an actress.

Come on, Garnet. Of course we want to be actresses. (Garnet can be a bit stupid and shy at times. She doesn't think we'll ever make it as flashy film stars, but I keep telling her all we need is CONFIDENCE. She keeps going on now, saying she doesn't want to be a star. Well, that's crazy. She can't mean it. Who on earth wouldn't want to show off all day in front of the camera and go to swanky parties every night with all the other stars?)

We'll live in our own luxury condo with lots of flowers in every room and huge boxes of chocolates to dip into whenever we want, and we'll wear ruby-red sequin gowns and ruby jewelry to match—okay, okay, Garnet, you can have garnets, only they're not as precious and valuable and sparkly, *are* they?

That's not what you wanted to say? Well, what *do* you want to say then? All right. You write your part now. Go on. Here you are. Get moving. You write about you.

I don't know what to put.

I'm not used to writing about me. It's always us. I do like writing, though. I was a little annoyed when Ruby found this beautiful red book and started scribbling all that stuff. I thought we could maybe use it to write down our plays. We've always played these pretend games together since we were little. We pretend to be other people and make things up. It used to seem so real that it would get mixed up with our ordinary life. It can still seem real for me, but Ruby often goofs off and won't play. She doesn't like going over and over a play—she just wants me to keep making up new ones for us. She doesn't seem to realize it's hard work. And if we keep starting on new plays then some of the best old plays get forgotten. I want to write them down properly to keep them safe.

I like making up plays and I don't mind acting them out when it's just Ruby and me and we're totally private and imagining it so it could almost be actually happening, but I can't bear real acting.

Ruby and I were twin sheep in the nativity play

when we were still in grade school and it was one
of the most truly awful experiences of my life.
   Not the most awful, of course.
   That was when

Look, you're not writing any of that sad stuff,
I won't let you. This is me again. Ruby. Garnet's
just gone off, all grumpy because I happened to
scratch her a tiny little bit when I snatched the
pen. I asked her nicely first. And it's my turn
now. You have to be able to take turns fairly
when you're twins.

That stuff she wrote is silly anyway. What's
the point of writing plays down in books? You
should *play* plays. And she's got to be an actress
because that's what we've always wanted to be,
and while we're still trying to get famous we can
do commercials and game shows on TV. Identical twins are a mega-novelty.

Garnet can't reject Fame just because of that
one unfortunate experience of being a sheep
when we were little.

She got so worked up and nervous when we
had to perform that she wet herself. Onstage. In
front of everyone. But it didn't really *matter.* I
don't know why she still gets all hot and bothered if I happen to bring it up. It was quite ap-
propriate, actually, because that's what real
sheep do all the time. They don't hang around

the stable with their back legs crossed, holding it in. They go all over the place. Which is what Garnet did. And everyone thought it was ever so funny. Except Garnet.

Got to go now. I can smell Sunday dinner. Roast beef and popovers, yummy yummy yummy in my tummy.

Ruby! You mean pig. You've told about me being the sheep!

Look, *you* were the one who mentioned it first. You went on and on about it.

Yes, but I didn't say what happened. It was my most painful and humiliating secret. And now you've told, Ruby.

I haven't *told*. I've written. And this accounts

book is secret. Just for us. We can write every-thing down in it. All our secrets.

Yes, but you haven't written down your secrets. You've written down mine.

Oh, quit fussing. Let's go and eat. I'm starving.

Gran's upset because Dad's very late getting back from his flea market and she's had his din-ner keeping warm in the oven for the last half hour and her popovers are going all sad and soggy.

Like some silly twin. Come on, Gran's calling.

Dad should have been back ages ago. He is all right, isn't he?

Of course he is. You are an old worrywort, Garnet. He'll have just bought up an entire bookstore, that's all, and he'll be having trouble stuffing them all into the car. You know what he's like.

Yes, but he's not usually as late as this. And he likes Gran's Sunday dinners as much as we do. What if he's had an accident?

Oh, Garnet, shut up. Coming, Gran.

Chapter 2

We haven't been able to write recently because tons and tons of stuff has been happening. And now I suppose I should write it all down and yet I don't know where to start. You have a try, Garnet. Go on.

I don't want to go on. I want to stop. No. I want to go backward. Back past the day Dad came back late from the flea market. Back past the ordinary-us-twins-and-Dad-and-Granny-day-after-day part. Back through the awful time when Mom died and

STOP IT STOP IT STOP IT

No, Ruby. We can't stop now. We've got to remember. And don't you see? We've got to make Dad remember. And then he'll stop seeing Rose.

Ah. All right. But tell it quickly. The part about Mom. Tell it as if it was a story and not real so that it won't hurt so much.

Once upon a time a man called Richard fell in love with a girl called Opal. Opals are beautiful stones that shine all different colors. But some say opals are unlucky. This girl Opal was beautiful and she shone and Richard knew he was lucky lucky lucky to have met her.
Richard loved Opal. He sometimes kidded around and called her Oh Pal. Because he said she was his pal. And he gave her an opal ring.

Where's that ring? Remember how we used to be allowed to try it on? But I haven't seen it for ages. Oh no. Oh, Garnet, you don't suppose Dad will give it to *Rose?*

No! Of course not. Gran's got it safe in her jewelry box and she says we'll get it when we're grown up.

Which one of us? It ought really to be me, seeing as I'm the oldest. But I'll let you borrow it sometimes. If you're careful.

I'm the careful one. Look, you've interrupted my story now.

Go on then. You got to the ring part. Dad gave Mom the ring.

Richard gave Opal a beautiful opal ring, milky white but with all different pinks and blues and greens and purples, sparkling like magic whenever it caught the light.

They got their own apartment.

They got married.

They had twin daughters.

Which is which? I'm that one, the baby with Mom.

No, that's me. You're the baby with Dad. I drew it so I should know.

Well, I can't help that. The baby with Mom is the biggest baby, you just look and see. And *I* was the biggest, we both know that. That's baby Ruby.

It doesn't matter anyway. Okay, you're the baby with Mom.

Right. Well. Mom held you too, of course. She held me and then she held you, and Dad held me and then

And then we grew up a bit and we could toddle around and we didn't need to be held. Though we still had cuddles with Mom. We sat on her lap. Both of us together. I can remember.

You're just remembering that photograph. Hey, let's stick it in the accounts book.

It's not just the photo. I can remember. She felt so soft and yet her arms could hold you so tight you felt safe. And there was her flowery smell, and her curly hair tickled. She tickled us too, remember? This little piggy went to market and then she'd tickle us and we'd get all squirmy. Remember that, Ruby?

(She's gotten all quiet. She can't stand remembering because it makes her so sad and she can't stand being unhappy. She won't ever cry. That's one of the few ways people tell us apart. If one of us has turned all red and watery-eyed then it's me.

I think I might cry a bit when I write this next part. I'll go back to doing it like a story. And I'll scribble it down ever so quickly.)

The twins started school, and Opal and Richard went to work and on the weekend they did fun things like going swimming and shopping and they had days at the seaside. All the normal nice family things. But then everything stopped being normal and nice. Opal got a little sick. Then she had to go into the hospital. She was all right for a while after that. But then she got sick again. She couldn't work anymore. She lay on the sofa at home. Gran had to pick up the twins from school. Richard stopped working and looked after Opal. But she couldn't get better. She died. So they stopped being a family.

There. I've written it. Do you want to read what I said, Ruby? No, she doesn't. It was three years ago. When we were seven. But we're ten now and it's all right again. We can't ever be our old family but we're a new family now. Gran lives with us and she's not like a mother, but then no one can ever be like a mother to us. NO ONE. NO ONE AT ALL. ESPECIALLY NOT STUPID FRIZZY DIZZY ROSE.

This is Rose.

22

No, THIS is Rose.

Yes, that's Rose. Only she's even worse than that. What does Dad see in her? He's the only one who likes her. Gran doesn't like her one little bit.

Gran's face when Dad turned up with Rose that Sunday! We all just stared at her. And Dad came out with all this blather about how she'd helped him when his bag of books broke, and then surprise surprise her car wouldn't start so he'd given her a lift and they'd stopped at a coffee bar for a quick cappuccino on the way home and she was all set to have a sandwich for her lunch and Dad said he'd got a genuine roast-beef-and-all-the-trimmings waiting for him at home and she went Oooh it's ages since I had a real Sunday dinner like that so guess what, folks. He brought her back. To share our Sunday lunch.

"There's no problem, is there, Gran?" Dad said.

"No, of course not. Do come and sit down at the table, Rose. There's plenty of food. I'm afraid the beef will be a bit overdone and I can't take pride in my popovers today. They *were* lovely and light and fluffy, but . . ."

"But I waylaid your son-in-law and kept him out on the town and messed up your meal," said Rose, and she actually laughed. "Sorry about that," she said, though she didn't look the *slightest* bit sorry.

Gran had to smile back at her through gritted teeth like it was funny.

We didn't smile, though, did we, Garnet?

She couldn't take the hint, though. She chatted away to us about TV programs and pop records and stuff, as if she'd known us years and years. And she kept trying to remember which of us was which.

"Now, you're Garnet, right?" she said to me. "And you're Ruby," she said to Garnet.

"Yes," we said. "Right."

"Wrong," said Dad, laughing uneasily. "That's Ruby. And that's Garnet. They're a pair of jokers. Even Gran and I get confused sometimes."

"Speak for yourself," Gran said huffily. "I'm sorry the beef was so dry. Though it would have been cooked just right an hour or so ago. Anyway. Apple pie and ice cream? Help me clear the plates, girls."

We helped her clear and when we came back with the dessert plates I sat in Garnet's chair and she sat in mine. Rose was none the wiser. She chattered away to me, calling me Garnet, and she jabbered stuff to Garnet, calling her Ruby.

"Yes, I'm beginning to be able to tell you apart," she said. "You're Ruby. And you're Garnet. Yes. Right."

"Well. Not *quite* right," said Dad. He came out with this false ho-ho-ho as if it were a great joke. "Stop teasing poor Rose, twins. I'm afraid they've swapped seats. They're always doing it.

I'd just call each girl 'Twin' and be done with it, Rose."

"Oh, I think that's awful," said Rose. "I couldn't stand that if I were a twin."

Well, certainly twin Roses would be *awful*.

"You're two separate people who just happen to be sisters, aren't you, Garnet and Ruby. Or Ruby and Garnet. Whichever. I'm all mixed up."

"We like being called Twin," I told her.

"That's what they call us at school," said Garnet.

"We *are* twins . . . ," I said.

"So we like . . . ," said Garnet.

"Being called . . . ," I said.

"Twins," we said simultaneously.

Rose raised one eyebrow and gave a little nod. "Okay, okay," she said. "Got it."

She stopped trying to be so chummy with us then. She tried complimenting Gran on her apple pie but Gran stayed as dried up as the dinner and barely said a word. So Dad did all the talking, on and on, saying all this silly stuff and making faces and telling stupid stories.

He didn't sound like Dad at all.

It was as if *he'd* swapped with a new twin dad.

He didn't go back to being our dad even when we'd got rid of Rose at last.

"Well, what did you think of her?" he asked eagerly.

I looked at Garnet. She looked at me. I raised

26

one eyebrow. She raised one too. Then we both turned sideways and pretended to be sick.

"All right, all right. You've done enough clowning around for one day," Dad said crossly.

"Yes, don't be so rude, Ruby and Garnet," said Gran—but she didn't sound a bit cross.

"Did you like Rose, Gran?" Dad asked.

"Well. She seems nice enough. I suppose. A bit . . . pushy, inviting herself to lunch like that."

"No, I invited her," said Dad. "I didn't think you'd make such a big deal out of it, actually. You've always said you wished I'd socialize a bit more, bring a few friends home, not stay so wrapped up in the past."

"Yes, dear. And I mean that. I'm only too pleased that you want to bring people back. Though if you could have just phoned to give me a bit of warning. . . . And you do want to be a bit careful with that type of woman."

"What do you mean, *type?*" said Dad, really angry now.

"Now, Richard, don't get in such a silly state," said Gran, as if he were our age. "It's just that she seems a little too eager. She's never set eyes on you before today and yet she's all over you, trying to act like one of the family."

"I've known Rose for months, if you must know," said Dad. "She's got her own bric-a-brac booth in the arcade—we're always bumping into each other at flea markets. I've always wanted to get to know her better—she's so bubbly and warm and friendly. I don't know how you can talk about her like that—she's a lovely girl."

"Girl!" said Gran. "She'll never see thirty again."

"Well, neither will I," Dad shouted. "And it's about time I started making the most of my life, okay?"

He stormed out of the house, slamming the door. There was a horrible silence after he'd left. Garnet got hold of my hand and squeezed it tight. She looked like she was going to cry. *Gran* looked like she was going to cry too.

We were all shocked by the fight. We don't ever have fights in our family.

It's all that Rose's fault.

Yes, it's all Rose's fault. She started all the

changes. She comes every Sunday now. And in the week sometimes. And Dad goes out with her in the evenings and when they come back in the car, they KISS.

I hate changes. I want every day to be the same. I've always been this way, even before Mom died.

I couldn't stand our first day at school.

Everybody stared at us because we were different. And the whole day was different. We couldn't play our own games and talk in our own private language. It felt like we couldn't even be twins, be-

cause the teacher sat me on one side of the class-room and Ruby on the other. She said it was so she could tell us apart.

I felt as if she'd somehow torn us apart. I didn't feel a whole person at all. I felt like a half, as if an arm and a leg and most of my head were on the other side of the room stuck to Ruby. I didn't know how to think without her.

Well, naturally. I'm the oldest. I'm the *dominant* twin. That's what they call the one that's born first. That's me. I'm the Big Cheese. You're just the Little Crumb.

You didn't like us being separated either, Ruby. You didn't cry

You did.

but you were ever so naughty and so we got sent to the principal and she said, "Why are you so unhappy, Garnet? Why are you so naughty, Ruby?" and we said, "We want to sit together." And she said, "Is that all? Simple!"

And it was simple. We sat together. I didn't cry anymore. And Ruby wasn't naughty. Well, she was, but not so much.

But it still took me ages and ages to get used to school. But now it's okay. Everyone's so used to us they don't stare. We're just The Twins. That's the way we want it. We sit together in every class. We're always partners. We sit next to each other at lunch. We even go to the rest room together.

We're good at schoolwork. We sometimes come out on top, especially when we have to write stories or do a project.

But we like Drama best. We're absolutely fabulous at Drama. Well. *I* am. Garnet goes all red and gets her words mixed up.

Don't start, Ruby.

Well, you do. Only you wouldn't if you'd stop being so shy. I don't know why you're so shy. *I* never feel shy.

Look, I just want to write about

You've been writing for ages and ages and you keep gabbing on about us back in grade school and who's interested in baby stuff like that? Write about what's happening now. All the horrible parts.

Well, give me the pen.

Say please then. Hey! Get off!
"Are you two girls having a fight?"
That's Gran. She's seen us snatching the pen from each other.
"You can share nicely if you try. Now you're going to have to remember all I've taught you when you go. *She's* not the type to worry about good manners."
"Oh, Gran. I don't want to go!" I said, and I flung myself onto her lap.

"Watch my hip! And my knee! Ruby, you big
lump, get off me," said Gran—but she cuddled
me close all the same.

*"Can I come and join in the cuddle too?" I
asked.*

*I sat on the arm of the chair so I didn't hurt
Gran's other hip and knee, but she reached out
and pulled me right onto her lap.*

We clung tight. I started crying.

*"Stop it, Garnet," said Ruby, and she pinched
me hard. Her face was all screwed up. She was
scared I'd make her start crying, even though she
never cries. Gran's eyes were all watery too.*

*"Dear oh dear," she said, sniffling. She patted
us with her poor hands, the fingers all slipping
sideways with arthritis. She fumbled up the*

sleeve of her cardigan for her hankie and mopped my face and hers, and then pretended to blow Ruby's nose.

"We'd better turn off the waterworks. I don't want a puddle in my chair," said Gran.

"Oh, Gran, please please please come with us," Ruby begged.

"Now don't you start, young Ruby. You know it's all settled and decided."

"But we'll miss you so, Gran!" I said, nuzzling into her warm woolen chest.

"And I'll miss both of you, my girls. But you can come and stay with me on visits—you can sleep at either end of the sofa and bring your sleeping bags—and I'll maybe come to this new place for Christmas."

"Not maybe. You've got to come."

"We'll see. Of course, there's probably no point. She doesn't have a clue about cooking. She probably won't even bother to have a turkey."

"So why can't we all come to you for Christmas, Gran, and then we can have Christmas dinner the way you do it, with cranberry sauce and little sausages and chestnut stuffing, yummy yummy," said Ruby.

"That oven in my new place is so small it would be hard to cook a chicken in it," said Gran. "Sorry, pet. No more Christmas dinners."

"No more roast potatoes with special crispy bits and Christmas cake with little silver charms and

traffic-light Jell-O, red and yellow and green," Ruby wailed.

"I think you're going to miss my cooking more than you'll miss me," said Gran, shaking her head. "Come on now, you're both squashing me something awful. You'd better get back to your writing. Is it something for school?"

There's no point doing anything for school. Because we won't be going there much longer. We've got to go to a new school. In a new place. In a new life. And we're going to hate it.

It's all her fault. We hate her. WE HATE HER.

Yes. We hate her. It all started when Dad met

Rose. She kept coming around upsetting us. Barging in. Changing things.

She changed Dad. It isn't just the way he acts, all loopy and lovey-dovey, yuck yuck yuck. She's changed his clothes. He always used to wear just ordinary Dad clothes. Sweaters. Trousers. Suits and white shirts on weekdays, with stripey ties. She started with the ties. She bought him this bright red flowery number.

Then it was Marilyn Monroe. And Mickey Mouse. Dad looked like a cartoon himself in all these stupid ties. She didn't stop there. Oh no.

Would you believe, Donald Duck underpants!

At least they were hidden under his trousers. She started on his shirts next. Green stripes. Red checks. Blue polka dots.

She said they brightened up his dull old suit.

She was worse with his weekend clothes. She made him give his tracksuit and his comfy old corduroys to the thrift shop. She said they were old man's clothes. She's turned Dad into a new man. A new stupid trendy jerk of a dad in black jeans and denim jackets and lumberjack shirts.

She even calls him a new name. Rick. It's Rick this, Rick that. Sometimes it's even Ricky. It's enough to make you feel sicky.

Gran can't stand it either.

"His name's *Richard*," she hissed one day.

"We've always called him Richard. No one ever calls him Ricky or Rick."

She said it in the sort of voice that makes Garnet squirm. But Rose isn't the squirmy kind. She just smiled.

"*I* call him Rick," she said.

Gran scowled and sucked her teeth.

"Oh dear," said Rose sympathetically. "Is the pain really bad today?"

Rose is the Pain.

But Gran is in pain too. Her arthritis has gotten really bad. Sometimes she can't even get out of bed and Ruby and I have to help her. And it

*takes her ages and ages to get down the stairs
with her hip. And up the stairs to the bathroom.
And when she's in her chair she gets stuck and we
have to heave, Ruby one side, me the other.*

How is she going to manage without us?

*She's moving to sheltered housing. We thought
that meant she was being housed in a bus shelter.*

*It's not as bad as that. It's a little apartment on
the ground floor and she's going to have a Home
Help and an Alarm Button.*

*I feel as if I have an Alarm Button inside me
and it's going off all the time.*

We're moving too. Garnet and me. And Dad.
And *Her.* Dad lost his job. It's called Being
Downsized. Dad said he didn't care. He'd always
hated that boring old office. But he looked a bit
shocked all the same.

"So how are you going to manage without your boring old salary?" said Gran, sniffing. "Oh, Richard, you're such a fool. How could you spoil all your chances like this? And you've got the twins to think of too."

"It wasn't my fault," he said.

"You've never shown the right attitude. And since you've taken up with that Rose, you've turned into . . . into a *hippie*."

"Oh, for goodness sake—"

"Those silly ties and shirts were the last straw. Of course they got rid of you. So what are you going to do now? Have you looked at the Help Wanted ads in the papers?"

"I don't want that sort of job anymore," said Dad. "I've been thinking. They're giving me quite a bit of cash as my severance pay. It's my chance for a whole new start. We could sell out here, get a little shop in the country somewhere. A bookshop. You've always gone on and on at me to sell some of my books!"

"You're talking nonsense," said Gran. "Well, count me out."

Count us out too, Dad! Garnet and me. We don't want any part of this.

We don't want to move to a silly old shop in the country! We don't want to leave Gran. We don't want to leave all our friends. We don't want to leave our school. We don't want to leave our old lives. We don't want to live with you. Not if it means we've got to live with *her.* Because she's coming too. Rose.

We wish she'd get greenfly and mildew and wilt.

Chapter 4

If our writing's a bit shaky, it's because we're doing this account in the van.

We feel shaky. Our whole lives have been shaken up.

Dad really has bought a bookshop! He didn't

even take us with him to check it out first. He went away for the weekend with Rose, and when he came back he said, "Guess what! I've bought a shop."

We just stared at him, stunned. He's been acting so crazy. Not like a dad at all. Especially not our dad.

We're used to him saying, "Guess what! I've bought another box of books."

But you don't buy a book*shop* just like that. You're supposed to hang around for months, getting it inspected and seeing lawyers.

"It's all simple," said Dad. "This sweet old couple are retiring and are happy to move out right away. If I can't sell our own house, I'll rent it to students for a while. Your gran's got her sheltered housing all worked out. Rose only rents her room, and she can shut up her booth in the arcade anytime, so she hasn't got any problems either."

We're the ones with the problems. Garnet and me.

We don't even get considered.

"Why didn't you take us with you to see if *we* like it?" I asked.

"You'll love it," said Dad. "The village is clear out in the country, beside a river, with hills all around. It's a real storybook place. There's a pond with puddleducks straight out of Beatrix

Potter. There's just this one street of shops. Ours is in the middle. We'll fit it out with shelves and Rose can have the window for her bric-a-brac. She's got all sorts of ideas for getting it fixed up. And there's plenty of room upstairs. You two can have the attic for your bedroom—you'll like that."

Sarah Crewe gets stuck in an attic in A Little Princess *and she has to act like a servant to all the girls in her school. Though at least she got to* stay *in her school.*

We've had to leave our school.
It was awful saying good-bye.

But it was much worse saying good-bye to

Ruby doesn't want to write it. She always leaves the worst part to me. I don't want to write it either.

Oh, Gran. We do miss you. We miss you ever so ever so much. You used to get mad and you were strict and sometimes you even smacked, but you didn't hurt because of your poor hands and you couldn't help being strict because you're old and you were only cross when we were naughty.

But we wish you were with us now. You could be cross and strict and smack all the time and we wouldn't mind a bit.

You didn't get cross and strict and smack when we took you to your new apartment. But you weren't all happy and smiley. You looked small and scrunched up and sad and it was awful.

We helped you put your chair and your china cabinet and all the rest of your stuff in your new room, but they didn't look right. They didn't look yours. It didn't look like a home.

This funny old man from next door came over to say hello and he gave you a bunch of flowers he'd grown in his garden. Dad teased you and said you'd got yourself a boyfriend already, but you wouldn't smile. And when Dad said he hoped you'd be really happy in your new place and he was sure it was all for the best, you just sniffed. You didn't say anything, but you looked at Dad

and it was as if you were shrieking: Who are you
kidding?

You didn't even kiss Dad properly good-bye, just
gave him your cheek. And we don't blame you either, Gran.

You kissed us. And we kissed you. Lots and lots.

We didn't talk to Dad either. We're still not speaking to him unless we have to. Or Rose. We don't need to. We can just speak to each other. In Twinspeak, so they can't understand.

Garnet and I have this special language. We've got lots of made-up words for things. Sometimes we don't use words at all, we use signs. Little tiny things like widening our eyes or putting our heads slightly to one side. We signal to each other and then both start a pretend coughing fit, or sneeze simultaneously, or shriek with manic laughter.

Rose isn't used to this. It drives her crazy.

"Knock it off," says Dad.

I glance at Garnet.

"Knock it off what, Dad?" we say simultaneously.

"Don't be sarcastic," says Dad, taking one hand off the steering wheel and swatting at us.

"How do they *do* that?" Rose asks.

"How do we do what?" we say together.

"Stop it! You're giving me the creeps. Can you really read each other's thoughts?" she says, shivering.

"Of course they can't," says Dad.

"Then how can they say the same thing at the same time in that weird way?" Rose says, peering at us.

"I don't know," says Dad, shrugging.

"*We* know," we say, and we raise our eyebrows and make our eyes glitter in a mysterious and mystic manner.

We wait until Rose turns around again and starts fiddling with the old van radio, trying to tune it to a station. I point to it and nudge Garnet. We both start singing loudly, our timing perfect.

Rose gasps.

"Cut it out, twins," says Dad sharply.

I turn my fingers into pretend scissors and make lots of cutting movements. Garnet does the same.

"Oh, very funny," says Dad, not at all amused.

When he's concentrating on the road, I change the scissors to a dagger and mime a sudden bloody attack on Rose. Garnet does likewise, only she's not quite quick enough. Dad sees, so Garnet shakes her arm quickly, making out she's got a cramp.

"What are you playing at, you two?" says Dad.

We blink at him and shrug.

Dad sighs with exasperation, and then takes one hand off the steering wheel and puts his arm around Rose.

I nudge Garnet and we both make a very rude noise.

Dad's hand tightens on Rose's shoulder, but he doesn't say anything. She doesn't say anything either. Neither do we. The radio keeps buzzing and fading and sounding funny.

I feel a bit like that too. Maybe I'm starting to feel carsick. Well, vansick. Ooh, good! If I'm going to throw up then I'll aim at Rose.

Ruby was sick. She managed to hit Rose. And me.

Only little splashes on you.

You're not supposed to be writing, in case you get sick again.

I did great, didn't I?

Yes, but I'd rather you didn't do it again. Rose used a whole box of tissues, mopping away. Dad had to stop at the next service station and we had to go to the ladies'. I washed and Ruby washed. Rose positively scrubbed and changed her sweater and jeans, scrunching the stained smelly stuff into a plastic bag.
"I think you two belong in the bag too," she

said, sighing. *"Look,* I *don't care if you act like id-iots, but you're really upsetting your dad."*

We didn't say anything. But Ruby smiled, even though she was still sick and shivery.

"Don't you want your dad to be happy?" said Rose, looking at Ruby and then at me.

Not with you!

"He's had a really tough time the last few years. You two were only tiny so you probably didn't re-alize, but he nearly went to pieces after your mother died."

We stared at her silently, hating her. How dare she! We felt like we were in little pieces too.

"It was really tough for him, but he kept on go-ing for your sake. He did his best to get along with your grandmother, even though she can be diffi-cult at times."

How does she have the nerve *to criticize our grandmother!*

"He didn't have any fun, he never went out any-where, he was always lonely," she said.

How could he possibly have been lonely? He had us!

"He kept slaving away at that boring old job in the city, even though it nearly drove him crazy. He was like this old old man even though he's barely thirty."

She's crazy. He's our dad. He is *old.*

"But now he's got this big chance. A whole new life. Something that he's always wanted. And he's

been like a little kid—so excited. But you two are spoiling it all. Can't you see that?"

Yes, we can see it. That's what we want. It's not us that's spoiling anything. She's got it all wrong. It's her. It's her it's her it's her.

Chapter

We're here. And we hate it.

Yes. We hate it.

It's the worst place in the whole world, and we're stuck here with the worst people. Stuck stuck stuck.

Well, the place itself isn't that bad.

Yes it is!

No, wait, Ruby. I don't mean the shop. Or the village. But the countryside itself is okay, isn't it? Especially the hills. I hated going for a walk with Rose and Dad, but when we were up in the hills and we saw all the sheep and the wild ponies and we got right to the top and we were almost up in the sky and we could see for miles and it felt like we could just step off the edge and fly—

Will you put a sock in it, Miss Arty-Farty Show-Off. All this sky-and-fly stuff! You sound like you're writing a poem for school. "My Day in the Country." Boring! And the country's boring too. Gray hills and gray fields and gray trees and gray rain.

Rose doesn't think much of it either. She's still all lovey-dovey with Dad, but we're wearing her down—and this certainly isn't her dream place to live. She got seriously fed up when I accidentally on purpose waved that branch near the clothesline and snagged all her stupid tights and the village store only sells pale beige old-lady styles. Old Rose could have sold her soul for a Sock Shop then.

She hates the supermarket too. Because it doesn't have any decent fruit or vegetables and the bread's sliced up in bags.

Yes, but Dad says he'll grow raspberries and

tomatoes and green beans in the garden and he's going to try making our own bread.

Give me a break, Garnet! Dad can't even make *toast*. Gran was always talking about how hopeless he was.

Dad says that was because she never let him try his hand at anything. She always said, "Come on now, out from under my feet, stop cluttering up my kitchen." Oh dear. We do miss Gran. We wish she were here.

No, we wish *we* were *there*. Instead of here in this hateful dump. We don't fit in.

Dad's shop doesn't fit in either. Especially now. The antiques shops are all painted white or cream or very pale beige. Dad's shop started off dirty white too, so he decided to brighten it up.

"I'm going to call it The Red Bookshop," he said. "Because of my three girls. Rubies are red, Garnets are red, and Roses are red. So let's go the whole hog and paint it red too."

He drove miles and miles to the nearest do-it-yourself store and came back with gallons of blinding scarlet paint. We were supposed to help Rose wash the front of the shop and scrape the peeling paint, but after about ten minutes of scrubbing and sloshing, Ruby threw her sponge in the bucket and said, "We're fed up with this game," and sauntered off.

So I threw my sponge in the bucket too, and sidled after my sister.

"Hey, come back, you lazy dogs," Rose shouted, and she threw a sponge at us.

It bounced off Ruby, still sopping wet. Ruby took hold of it and aimed. She's a very good aimer. It caught Rose full in the face.

We ran clear away then. We walked around and around the village and up and down the stream and then we went down by the river but it was too muddy and we weren't wearing our boots and I slipped and got mud all over my bottom. It looked AWFUL. And Ruby made it worse because she kept laughing at me. I tried to rub the mud off with grass but it was useless.

I started to cry and Ruby got cross.

"Why do you always have to be such a baby?" she said. "Look, it's your own fault for slipping like that. And it doesn't matter anyway—they're only your old jeans. And she can't tell us off because she's not our mother or any part of our family. So stop sniveling."

"I can't go back through the village like this. People will look at me and laugh."

"No they won't. They won't even notice, honest," said Ruby.

She wasn't being honest. They did notice. This crowd of kids fishing by the bridge saw us and stared. First of all because we were strangers. Second because we're twins. But then they saw the gunk all over my jeans and then they really stared. And sniggered. And shouted horrible vulgar suggestions.

Ruby caught me by the wrist and gave me a little shake to stop me from crying again. She marched us straight up to them instead of skulk-

ing away, like I wanted. Her face was as red as her name.

"What's so funny?" she said when we were right up close to them. She made me say it too. "What's so funny?" we said in unison.

They were mostly around our age, but some were bigger. Ruby didn't care.

Some of the littler kids stepped backward. They weren't just worried about Ruby. It was me too. Because we were walking in step and talking exactly together and when we do that lots of people find it really spooky.

The bigger boys weren't easily fazed, though. One fat one with silly sideways hair said something impolite and horrible and they all laughed again.

"Ooh! Being covered in mud is funny, is it?" said Ruby.

"Funny, is it?" we said together.

Then Ruby looked at me and looked at the muddy grass and I knew what she was going to do. I knew I had to do it too. We bent, we stuck our hands into the mud, we straightened up— and while they were still all gawking at us we went splat, right in their faces.

"Have a big laugh then," said Ruby—and we ran.

They started running after us, but we can be very speedy so we soon got clean away. Well. I wasn't clean. I was still covered in mud.

"But so are they!" Ruby spluttered breathlessly. "Their faces. Oh, Garnet, that was so glorious. Twin-grin!"

"Twin-grin," I echoed obediently, though I didn't really feel like smiling.

We have this little grinning ritual whenever we're really pleased about something. Ruby puts her fingers at the corners of my mouth and turns it into a huge grin, while I reach out at the same time and do the same to her.

I managed to stay grinning like a Halloween pumpkin, but I kept looking behind me all the same, in case those kids might be creeping up on us.

"Relax. They'll have gone back to their stupid fishing," said Ruby, sensing that I was still scared.

"Maybe. But they'll still be out to get us sometime, won't they," I said stiffly, trying to keep my grin in place.

"Well, we'll get them back," said Ruby airily. "Especially that big blobby one."

"But they'll all start hating us then. And we've got to go to school with them, haven't we," I said. My grin wavered and then drooped.

"We won't go to this dumb old school. We'll sneak off by ourselves," said Ruby.

"But they'll find out and we'll get into trouble," I said. "And we're in pretty big trouble now. We can't go home because Rose will get us, and we can't go down by the river because those kids will get us."

It looked like we were stuck forever, hiding up a little alleyway at the edge of the village. I leaned against the wall, the cold pebbly stuff scratching me through my T-shirt. My jeans were still wet and sticky with mud. My face ached with trying to smile. My eyes stung with trying not to cry again.

"Garnet?" said Ruby gently.

She put her arm around me and cuddled me close. I snuggled up against her and we held on tight to each other. Our shadows became Siamese.

"Perhaps we'd better go back to the bookshop," I said eventually.

"No, not yet. We've only been gone an hour or so. She'll just get angry. No, we have to stay away ages and ages, and then she'll be really worried. Better to stay away until Dad gets back, then he'll be worried too, and they'll maybe have a fight. Then when we do turn up they'll be so relieved we haven't been kidnapped or killed that they won't give us a hard time. Or not so much, anyway."

"But what are we going to do?" I wailed.
"We'll do one of our plays," said Ruby.
That made me cheer up. Ruby hasn't felt like playing one of our pretend games in ages.
So we had this really great game together.

And then, when we eventually slunk back to the shop, Rose didn't get cross with us.
She'd done all the front of the shop by herself, but she didn't tell on us to Dad. She even washed out my jeans for me without a fuss. Gran would have gone nuts.

What's the matter with you, Garnet? Have *you* gone completely nuts? Is this Let's Love Rosy-Posy Day?

No. I can't stand her, you know that. But I'm just trying to write a truthful account, that's all. In our accounts book.

Well, I think we should give a good account of ourselves. And a bad account of everyone else. That's much more fun.

Rose was okay when that woman in the quilted jacket and the droopy dog came to complain about the red paint.

Dad looked like he was going to burst into tears, but Rose went "Oh B-B-B-R-R-R-R-R-R-R-R-R!*," blowing this giant raspberry and said it was our shop and we could paint it whatever color we want and that the video store two doors down with all its posters didn't exactly add to the authentic Victorian charm of the village anyway. So the bossy lady went off in a huff and flounced out with her floppy dog and we were all laughing—*

Yes, but Rose wasn't really that clever, because how many real customers has Dad had?

Well, there was the man who wanted the gardening book . . . and the lady who wanted all the astrology guides . . . lots of ladies . . .

Yes, but they only spend a dollar at a time!

That priest came. And he bought a Bible—the big one with pictures that costs oodles.

And that's about *it*. They don't want to come, the villagers. They don't like us. Or they don't like books. Or both.

Yes, but Dad says he's really after the tourist

trade. The people who come on weekends. And vacationers.

Who'd ever want to spend a vacation in this old dump? All right, the shop did get busy last Saturday and Sunday, but hardly anybody *bought* anything.

There were the hikers and they left mud all over the place.

There were the bikers and they dripped ice cream everywhere.

And there was that family who asked to use the toilet.

None of that bunch bought a thing.

One of the bikers bought an old Beano *comics annual.*

Oh, big deal. I'm telling you, Garnet. Dad's going to go broke in six months.
Come on, let's play. Make the most of our free time. Because we're starting at our new school on Monday, yuck yuck yuck.

Chapter **6**

It's awful. We knew it would be. It's like a little toy school. There's hardly any playground. There aren't any computers. There isn't even a television set. The teacher writes stuff up on a blackboard and we sit at these dinky little desks with lids and inkwells. It's like the sort of classroom you see in a cartoon.

Miss Debenham isn't a bit like that, Ruby! This
is Miss Debenham.

Yes, and she made me feel positively sick and
squirmy inside when she stood us in front of the
class and introduced us—as if we *needed* intro-
ducing anyway. We're famous in this dreary
dump of a village. Everyone knows us.

Especially Jeremy Treadgold and his gang.

Fancy that big blob being in our class. It's a
wonder he can cram himself into the teeny-
weeny desk. Imagine having to sit next to him.

I'm glad we can sit together, anyway. Miss

Debenham asked us what we'd prefer. Teachers don't usually ask you stuff like that, they just tell you what they want you to do. And I like some of the lessons, like when we had to write about twins.

You can be a real smarmy little creep sometimes! I had it all figured out.

THE GOOD THINGS ABOUT BEING A TWIN

Everything

THE BAD THINGS ABOUT BEING A TWIN

Nothing

And then you were supposed to do your mirror-writing trick. It would have been so excellent:

THE GOOD THINGS ABOUT BEING A TWIN

Everything

THE BAD THINGS ABOUT BEING A TWIN

Nothing

It would have been PERFECT. An answer, and a twin answer. Identical, like us.

But oh no, Miss Suck-up-to-the-teacher-smarty-farty has to write all that garbage.

THE GOOD THINGS ABOUT BEING A TWIN

There are lots and lots of good things about being a twin. You're never alone, you've always got a best friend to talk to and play with. You can have all sorts of special secrets and make up wonderful games that no one else can ever understand. You can say things together and do things together so that you can have twice the power.

THE BAD THINGS ABOUT BEING A TWIN

There aren't many bad things about being a twin. Just occasionally it might be peaceful to be alone. Not to have to talk or make up games or listen to secrets. Just to be yourself. Not part of anyone else. You.

Very *bad,* Garnet! Do you *really* want to be left alone? Okay, I'll run off the next time that Big Blob tries to get us.

Oh, that was so awful! He crept up on us with huge wiggly worms in both hands, and I can't stand worms.

Well, I'm not absolutely enchanted with them myself. Especially not squirming down my

70

pullover. But I got mine out. I shoved it straight down the Big Blob's trousers!

Judy said he once put a worm down her neck too. Judy just about went bananas. She said—

I'm not the slightest bit interested in Judy and what she said. I don't know why you wanted to go off with her.

She's very nice, Ruby, she really is. And I didn't go off with her, you know that. Miss Debenham said she wanted us to do this big Noah's Ark painting to brighten up the classroom wall and she was going around the whole class asking them which animal they wanted to paint, and I kept hoping nobody else would pick giraffes, be-

cause they're our favorite animal, so when she got to us I said, "Giraffe" quick. And Miss Debenham smiled at you too and said, "And you'll do a twin giraffe, right, Ruby?"

So I said, "Wrong, Miss Debenham. I don't want to paint any stupid old giraffe."

But why did you say that? And why did you have to choose a flea for your animal?

Simple. One little blob. Flea finished. And if you'd only shut up and waited for *me* to answer old Dumbo Debenham, you could have done a flea too. Then we could have just sat around for the rest of the class. But oh no, you have to go off with that ghastly Judy girl and paint stupid giraffes with her.

I didn't go off—well, not deliberately. I couldn't help it that Judy said she wanted to do a giraffe too. And I tried to back out, you know I did. But Miss Debenham said, "No, come on, Garnet, you said you'd like to do a giraffe. So you can do the giraffes with Judy. Never mind what Ruby wants to do."

Yes, never mind *me*.

Oh, Ruby. Don't be like that.

I'll be exactly how I want. If you want to pal around with Judy then fine, you go off with her.

I don't want to pal around with her.

So why did you let her tag along with us at recess then? Going gab gab gab until I felt like punching her in the mouth.

Well, what could I do? I couldn't tell her to go away.

I could.

You did. You were ever so rude to her. And I keep telling you, Ruby, she's fun, she really is— you'd like her if you'd get to know her.

I'm not going to get to know any of them. Okay. You go and have wonderful fun with your new friend. Pal around with her all you like. Just don't expect to pal around with *me*.

Ruby! Let's not quarrel. I hate it so. Ruby, come back. Please.

Chapter 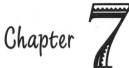 7

Ruby?

I can't stand *it when Ruby won't talk to me. It's as if most of me is missing. As if my own mouth won't work, my own hands won't hold.*

She's right. I was crazy to write that stuff about being a twin. It's awful being on your own.

Ruby wouldn't talk to me all yesterday evening. When I tried saying anything she put her hands over her ears and went Bla-bla-bla so she couldn't hear.

After we'd had supper, Ruby went up to our room and started reading an old Beano comics annual. I said I was sorry, but she didn't look up. I tried putting my arm around her but she wriggled away. I took hold of the book to make her look at me but she grabbed it back and hit me on the head with it. It hurt a lot, but that wasn't really why I was crying.

Ruby didn't take any notice at all.

My nose started to run so much that I had to go get a tissue. Rose saw me before I could mop myself up.

"Oh, sweetie," she said, and she pulled one of her chiffony scarves off her neck and wiped my nose with it. "Hey, I'm just running over to that video store because there's nothing good on TV tonight. Come and help me choose a good film, eh?"

I didn't know what to do. I knew Ruby would

*never forgive me if I cozied up to Rose. But it
didn't look like she would ever forgive me anyway.*

*"Come on, we'll get some chocolates too," said
Rose. She rubbed her tummy. "I've put on a good
five pounds since we got here. Still, never mind,
eh?"*

*I wanted to go with Rose. Ruby might not even
know unless she looked out of our window. No,
who was I kidding? It's like Ruby can look
through a little window straight into my head.*

*"I'd better not," I mumbled to Rose. "I mean, I
don't feel like it."*

*"You don't always have to do what Ruby
wants," Rose said.*

*She can tell us apart now. Unless we deliber-
ately trick her. She thinks she's getting to know
us. But she can't ever really understand. I don't
always get it myself. But I do have to do what
Ruby wants. Because if I don't, this happens. And
it's so horrid.*

*Rose usually chooses love films with big hunky
men, but this time she brought back* The Railway
Children. *It's one of my all-time favorite films,
but generally when we watch it Ruby goofs off
and makes fun of all the accents and at the end
when Bobbie runs to her father at the station and
it's so lovely, Ruby makes gagging noises and
switches it off before it's finished.*

*Dad raised his eyebrows a bit when he saw
which film it was, but he didn't say anything. He*

usually sits on the sofa with Rose, but this evening he sat in the armchair and he caught hold of me and sat me on his lap while Rose put her feet up on the sofa, a box of chocolates balanced on her tummy. She kept throwing Dad and me chocolates. I said I wasn't very hungry thanks, but Dad popped my favorite chocolate fudge into my mouth as I spoke and I couldn't really spit it out.

They were being awfully nice to me, but it didn't work. The chocolate didn't have any taste. The Railway Children *got started but I couldn't really watch it. I kept glancing up at the ceiling, at Ruby crouched up above us all on her own.*

"Why don't we ask if she feels like coming down now?" Rose said.

Dad and I looked at each other. Rose certainly doesn't understand Ruby yet.

Rose went up anyway. She left a couple of chocolates beside Ruby. They weren't touched when I came to bed.

Ruby and I always share the bathroom and do

synchronized toothbrushing, but Ruby barged straight past me and slammed the door in my face. When we got into our nighties in the bedroom she seemed to be staring straight through me, as if I didn't exist. That was exactly the way I felt.

When we were in bed with the light off I kept whispering to her, but she wouldn't answer. I lay awake for ages and ages and ages. In the middle of the night I slipped out of my bed and climbed in beside Ruby. She was snoring softly, deep in a dream, but she still wouldn't cuddle up and after a while I crept back to my own bed.

I think I slept a bit but now I'm wide awake again, even though it's not really morning.

I think Ruby's awake too.

Ruby?

She's still not speaking.

But I know what to do now.

I did it. And we're friends again now, aren't we, Ruby?

Yeah. Okay, okay. Get *off* of me, Garnet!

Make friends, make friends, never never break friends?

I said it, didn't I?

Write it too. Write it down here, in the accounts book. Write that you'll never break friends with me again.

I will never break friends with my twin sister and best friend Garnet Barker.

Oh, you've really written it! And put: I swear.

I swear my twin sister and best friend Garnet

Barker is driving me completely batty with all this sloppy junk, and if she doesn't shut up soon I might well go back on my promise.

You can't do that. No backsies.

I was only teasing, stupid. Here, what's all this drivel you've been writing? Whimpering on about me for page after page?

Don't look at it now. You're right. It was just garbage.

So you had chocolate fudge downstairs, did you?

I didn't mean to. I just had my mouth open and—

Oh, well. I might as well eat up my chocolates too. One . . . Yum yum yum.

And two . . . Gobble, gobble, gobble. Don't look at me like that. You had yours last night.

Only one.

Well look, here . . .

It's all chewed and slobbery!

Well, we're twins, aren't we? Your slobber is the same as my slobber. My drool is the same as your drool. My spit is the same as your spit.

Your spit is a lot splashier than mine.

Hey, wasn't it great today when we got Jeremy Blob splat-splat! Oh boy oh boy! That was the most terrific supersonic idea of mine, eh? Going up to him in the playground and saying stuff ever so ever so softly so he shakes his head and screws up his face. "What?" he says. "I can't hear you."

So we go, "Then wash your ears out" and you spit . . . SPLAT. And *I* spit . . . SPLAT. In his ears.

I wish Miss Debenham hadn't been walking across the playground just then. She wasn't very pleased either when I said I didn't want to finish my giraffe and I did a twin flea to match yours. And Judy was a bit fed up too, because now she's stuck doing one and three-quarters giraffes by herself.

Still, we don't care, do we?

It doesn't matter, so long as we've got each other.

So now school's a piece of cake, because Garnet and I don't do anything. We just sit looking blank when Dumbo Debenham calls on us. Or I write the barest minimum and Garnet does mirror writing. Or we copy everything twice—two columns of addition, two maps, two fact-sheets, because we say everything's got to be doubled because we're a double ourselves.

"Double trouble," said Dumbo Debenham, and she sighed and tried separating us, Garnet right at the back of the class and me at the front.

It didn't work. Garnet just had to keep her eye on me. I'd tilt my head one way, and that was the signal to sneeze simultaneously. Or I'd tilt my head the other way and we'd both tip our books off the desk. Or I'd nod very slightly and we'd both stand up and say in unison, "Please may I go to the toilet, Miss Debenham?" and then we'd walk out keeping step, me first, Garnet second, left right, left right, our arms swinging right left, right left, and then when I gave the slightest little cough we'd toss our heads so that our braids would go left right, left right, over our shoulders.

And all the kids would stare with their mouths open.

We even spook Jeremy Blob!

But it looks like we're in double trouble with Dad. Dumbo Debenham phoned him and told on us!

"So why are you acting so stupidly at school?" Dad demanded.

"I think they act stupidly at home too!" said Rose.

"We only act—"

"Stupid—"

"To stupid—"

"People," we said.

But then Dad shook us. Hard. I thought he might even bang our heads together.

"Stop it! I won't have you talking to Rose like that. What's the matter with you? I just don't get it. You've always been such good girls. Well, you've had your moments, Ruby, but you've never ever behaved as badly as this before. And you've both always done so well at school. I've been proud of you. But now it sounds as if you're going out of your way to be as naughty and disruptive as possible. And you're not even trying to make friends with the other kids. Miss Debenham says you've got into fights with some of the boys—and you really upset one of the girls yesterday. Judy someone?"

That was great. She was carrying on with this boring boring Noah's Ark nonsense and she'd just got started doing the giraffe's long neck with brown paint, so I got Garnet and we did our wanting-to-wee double act and then as we went out we both bumped into Judy accidentally on purpose and her giraffe ended up with this amazing corkscrew neck. Shame.

I couldn't help sniggering just thinking about it, and Dad got madder than ever.

Garnet spoiled it because she started sniveling, as always. Then Dad sighed and said, "Why do you always have to copy Ruby, Garnet? You obviously tried hard at school at first. But now you're starting to be just as naughty as Ruby." And then he shook me a bit and said, "Why can't you ever copy Garnet, Ruby?"

But Garnet was okay.

"I don't copy Ruby," she said.

"I don't copy Garnet," I said.

And then I sniffed because I knew Garnet was just about to, and I rubbed my dry eyes and she rubbed her wet ones, and then Garnet knew I'd stare at Dad defiantly with my chin up so she did too.

It unnerved Dad, even though he's used to us. But Rose clapped her hands.

"They ought to go on the stage," she said.

"Well ha ha ha, we're going to," I said.

Garnet was a bit slow with her response this time. She only managed a ". . . going to," and she sounded a bit half-hearted. But I'm her other half. The oldest biggest bossiest half. We have to do what I say.

This is it! Our Big Chance!

We were sitting in the kitchen on Saturday, messing around. Dad was down in the shop. Rose had caught the early bus to town. We had the place to ourselves. Garnet mixed up some flour and water and started making dinky little dough twins.

She even braided their hair and gave them little laces in their sneakers.

I said I wanted mine to have Doc Martens— all the better for kicking, ha ha—and I tried to change their shoes, but they wouldn't go right. So I squashed my twin up and started all over again, but it just got all blobby. I turned it into Jeremy Blob instead, while Garnet made another me. Then I got some toothpicks and tortured Jeremy Blob until he stopped looking like a doughboy and turned into a porcupine.

I got fed up with dough then and folded up a newspaper and cut it out carefully the way Gran showed us once and then, when I unfolded it, there was this whole row of paper dolls. The newspaper just happened to be Rose's *Guardian* and she hadn't even opened it yet. Tough.

I got a felt-tip pen and started scribbling in eyes and mouths and buttons down the front of each little paper girl. I'm not artistic like Garnet. I don't care about being so finicky.

"I'm turning them all into twins," I said.

I did a smiley mouth for me and a little-o anxious mouth for Garnet, and then a smiley mouth for me and a . . .

And then I stopped, because I saw the word Twin on the paper doll. I read her skirt and then I dug around for the leftover paper to try to read the rest. I got out the transparent tape and started trying to stick the whole shebang back together again.

"Yes, Rose is going to want to read that when she gets back," Garnet mumbled, putting the finishing touches to the little dough me.

"Forget Rose reading it. *We've* got to read it!" I said, and I was so shaking with excitement that I stuck myself together with the tape. "Garnet, come take a look at this! Oh boy! No, oh *girl*. Oh *twin* girl!"

"Whatever are you babbling about?" said Garnet. "Hey, don't jerk. Look, you've made me mess up your braid now."

"Leave it. *Look*!"

I shoved the crumpled, taped sheet of paper in front of her nose.

WANTED: GIRL TWINS

Sunnylea Productions are going to turn Enid Blyton's much loved Twins at St. Clare's books into a children's television series. Auditions start Monday for the leading roles, the twins themselves, so any likely lively outgoing twin girls aged 10–14 with showbiz ambitions can show up at 10 Newlake Street, London W1, at nine o'clock.

"This is it, Garnet!" I shouted.

Garnet is usually a quick reader but she seemed to be taking her time getting through one small paragraph.

She was still holding the little dough me.

"Hey, watch out! You're spoiling me," I said.

Garnet squashed me into a little ball and then dropped me on the kitchen floor.

"No," she said.

"But it says 'lively.' I'm not a bit lively. I don't jump around like you, I just sort of flop in a corner. And I'm not outgoing. I'm as inwardbeing as you could possibly get."

"You'll be okay. Just copy me."

Why do I always have to copy Ruby?
I can't act.
I don't want to act.
I can't go to an audition in London! I can't say a lot of stuff with everyone watching. It'll be even worse than being a sheep. Why can't Ruby understand? She won't listen to me. She's flipping through The Twins at St. Clare's *right this minute, trying to choose which part we'll act out.*
Only I'm not going to act.
I can't can't can't act.

"What?"

"No. I can't."

"What do you *mean*? We can we can we can. Yes, all right, it's going to be difficult getting to London by nine o'clock. We'll have to get up ever so early. Rose will have to look after the shop herself while Dad drives us. Still, that'll be fun."

"*No.*"

"Yes. Now, we're going to have to work mega-fast preparing our audition number. Get the book, quick, and we'll learn one of the scenes."

"Ruby, I can't. I can't act for beans, you know I can't."

"Look, it'll be fine. I promise you won't wet yourself this time."

"Stop it. It's not funny. I don't *want* to be in showbiz. Look, you go if you want, but I'm not."

"Oh ha ha, very helpful. How can I audition as a twin by myself, eh? Take one of the little dough twins along with me? Don't be such a dope. Now, where's the book, we've got to get busy. Which twin is which? I'll be the one that says the most. We'll work it so you hardly have to say anything, okay?"

"No, Ruby, please, *please.*" Garnet started scrabbling at me, getting dough all over my sweater.

"We can't miss out on this, Garnet. It's our big chance. We've got to go for it."

Remember what Gran says? There's no such word as *can't*! Now stop scribbling and start spouting. We've got to be word-perfect by Monday!

It's okay! I don't have to act after all. Dad won't let us.

I can't believe he could be so Mega-Mean. He doesn't seem to see that this is our one big chance, tailor-made for us. He won't even take it seriously.

"Don't be silly, Ruby. As if I'd drive you all the way to London at the crack of dawn on Monday! And I don't want you and Garnet involved in any acting job while you're still children. I can't stand those simpering stage-school monsters. You're already enough of a show-off as it is."

What NERVE! He won't put himself out to help us achieve our all-time ambition

Your *ambition*

and yet look what we've had to do for him. We've had to leave Gran and all our friends and our old school and come and live in this horrible dusty old dump in the middle of the boring bleak rainy old country which is all mud and sheep and nothing else and he says we've got to have old Rosy Ratbag as our *mother.*

Stepmother. And Rose said she didn't see herself as a stepmother anyway, and she didn't want us to feel she was forever trying to slip us poisoned apples. She said she just wanted to be our friend.

Well, we don't ever ever ever want to be friends with her. Do we? *Do we, Garnet?*

I suppose not. No. But she's not really as bad as all that. And she said she didn't see why we couldn't go to the audition. She said she thought we'd walk away with the parts. She told Dad not to be so stuffy. She said she'd even get up early on Monday and drive us in the van.

Yes, but she didn't really mean it. She knew Dad would put his foot down and say no.

Still, she did stick up for us.

Look, what is this, the Rosy Ratbag Appreciation Society? You'll be writing a fanzine about her next. Save your appreciation for *us.*

Only we're not going to be in The Twins at St. Clare's.

Oh yes we are.

The talented gems of stage and screen, identical twins Ruby and Garnet Barker, who first sprang to stardom in the acclaimed television series, The Twins at St. Clare's.

Dad won't let us. He won't ever change his mind. He's like you. He won't take us.

I know he won't take us. So we'll take ourself.

What?

I'll fix it. We *can't* miss this chance. Come on, Garnet. Twin-grin. *Smile.*

Ruby won't be able to fix it—will she???

I DID FIX IT!

I prodded my brainbox into action and charged out on Saturday afternoon to arrange things. I phoned the station to check on train times.

I went into the video store and ordered a taxi for quarter past five on Monday morning. Mr. Baines the video man is also the taxi man. *And* he's also a nosy old goat who wanted to know why we were going to the station to catch the early train. I told him this story about it being Gran's birthday. He seemed to take it for granted that Dad was going to be visiting her too.

Then I went to the nearest antiques shop and tried to sell my silver locket and my wristwatch and a dopey old china baby doll that Gran gave me. I never liked it even when I was little. Garnet played with mine as well as hers. But the doll *was* mine. And the locket and the watch. But the antiques shop lady wouldn't buy them. She said I had to have my mother or father with me.

Well, I haven't *got* a mother. Or much of a dad.

I tried the next antiques shop. No go. And the last one. Useless.

But did I give up? Nope. I went to the flea market in the field by the river on Sunday morning. No one was very interested in my chain and my watch but I saw them get excited about the doll, even though they tried to act like they weren't interested. They offered me a ten like they were doing me a favor. I'm not stupid. I asked for seventy-five. Of course they didn't *give* me seventy-five. But they gave me thirty.

Which wasn't going to be enough for the taxi and the train fare, even with all our savings in our piggy bank, so when my alarm went off at four in the morning I sneaked downstairs while Garnet was still asleep and borrowed a bill or two out the till. It isn't really stealing if it's your own family, is it? If you're going to pay them back anyway? Well, all right, it is—but I *had* to.

Then I went and woke Garnet and we fumbled about in the dark getting ready, in our best clothes and then we crept downstairs and scarfed some cookies for breakfast and then stood outside the front door waiting for Mr.

Baines so that he wouldn't ring the bell and wake Dad or Rosy Ratbag. They were still sound asleep. I checked.

Mr. Baines was ten minutes late so I was in a bit of a tizzy in case we were going to miss the train, and then he held things up by asking where Dad was, and he's got this incredibly loud voice and I was sure he was going to wake everyone up. But I rose to the occasion. I told him this story about Dad having a tummy bug and being unable to travel, but Gran was so disappointed when he phoned her that he promised to send us on our own.

"Two little girls like you?" said Mr. Baines doubtfully, but I showed him my bulging purse and told him Gran was meeting us at the train, so he shrugged and said okay.

Garnet didn't say a word. She still seemed half-asleep. Then she went green in the taxi. *I'm* the one who gets travel sick, but I was perfectly okay. I even remembered to give Mr. Baines a tip, though I didn't think he really deserved it, being late and asking hundreds of questions all the way.

I bought the tickets for the train. Garnet wasn't with me. She was throwing up behind a bush. I was worried she might mess up her best jacket. You can't audition attractively with vomit all down your front. But she was very neat about it, though she looked greener than ever when she came back. Still, our jackets are green, so at least she matched.

She was all shivery, even on the train. I made her rehearse a bit and she got even more trembly and tearful.

"Don't you dare cry," I said. "You don't want to be all red-eyed and bleary at the audition."

She did cry some anyway, but I mopped her up in the ladies' room.

"You're not going to let me down, are you, Garnet?" I said very fiercely.

Sometimes you've got to be fierce to get what you want. But even I felt a bit timid when we got off the train because it was all so big and busy and we didn't know where to go and we asked someone where Newlake Street was and they'd never even heard of it, and I said we'd take the subway but we didn't know which line, or where, and we went down the escalator and then back up the escalator and then I saw a taxi sign and we still had some money in our purse so we took a taxi.

It turned out we didn't have quite enough money after all. The taxi driver got a bit nasty.

But I wasn't bothered about that. I was bothered about something else. I got out of the taxi and Garnet staggered out after me. And we stared. And hundreds of eyes stared back at us. Twin eyes. Twin after twin after twin after twin.

It was so weird *seeing so many twins. Ruby and I have seen identical twins before, obviously, but never* hundreds *of pairs. It was as if the whole world had split into two. I felt as if I was splitting too. We've always felt so different. Unique. Special. It's what made us* us. *But standing there in that street we were just part of the crowd. Totally ordinary. With nothing at all to make us stand out.*

"Let's go back home," I said to Ruby. "Look at them all. We don't stand a chance."

"Don't be so ridiculous," said Ruby furiously. "I keep telling and telling and telling you, this is our big chance. We're not giving up now. We'll show them all. We'll act better than any of them."

"But I can't act at all, *Ruby."*

She just gave me this terrible look, took hold of my arm, and marched me to the end of the very long line.

We passed big twins

little twins

pretty twins

plain twins

showy twins

shabby twins

girly-girly twins

tomboy twins

even real boy twins.

"They obviously haven't even read the book!" said Ruby dismissively. *"Unless they're going to put on gowns and wigs and play the parts in drag."*

"But look at some of the others. The ones with the big smiles and loud voices. I bet they've been to acting school," I said.

"Well, so what. I've done my best to school you in acting. Now come on, let's go over our parts."

"Not out here, in front of everyone," I said, agonized.

"Look, you're the one who needs lots of practice, not me," said Ruby. Then she pulled me close and muttered in my ear, *"We'll just do it in whispers, okay? And I've been thinking—we'll have to inject a little oomph into our act to make us stand out in front of all the others. So we'll still do the scene with the twins having a battle with Mam'zelle, but we'll act Mam'zelle too. Don't look so scared, I'll do her. I am good at doing zee French accent, ma cherie, oh la la, très bon."*

But it turned out we didn't get a chance to do any of our act. We had to wait hours and hours in the line and I was desperate to go to the bathroom so when we did eventually get inside the building I had to walk around with my legs crossed and we had to give our names and addresses and date of birth and school to this lady at a desk and then we went upstairs and I was scared I might really wet myself and it would be *the sheep situation all over again only worse but there were toilets along the corridor and a big dressing room where you were supposed to change only we didn't have anything to change into, 'cause we were wearing it. But Ruby pinched my cheeks to give me a bit more color and I fixed up our hair although my hands were trembling so much I could barely tie a knot and then we got into* another *line, waiting to get into the actual audition room.*

It got scarier and scarier and I had to dash back to the bathroom once or twice and even Ruby got fidgety and she kept staring around at all the other twins. They were rehearsing their routines and they all seemed so brilliant that Ruby started to frown and bite her nails.

"I didn't think that we might have to dance," she mumbled. "They don't do any dancing in the story, do they? Although maybe they're turning it into a musical? So if we're asked, we'll sing . . . er . . . not a pop song, they'll all do that. We could do 'My Bonnie Lies Over the Ocean' with hand gestures."

"I'm not singing, especially not with gestures!" I said. "You know we can't sing in tune, either of us."

"Well, we could just sort of say the words, with lots of expression," said Ruby relentlessly. "And if we have to dance, well . . . we'll just have to jump and jiggle a bit. Improvise. You copy me, okay?"

This was so obviously not okay that I didn't even bother to protest.

"We could work on a routine now, you know," said Ruby, hopping and skipping and kicking out one leg.

She kicked a little too enthusiastically, and there was an argument with the twins in front of us.

They were dressed up in wonderful old-fashioned school uniforms—gymsuits and baggy blouses and lisle stockings and strappy shoes. One of the lisle stockings had a little run in it now where it had connected with Ruby's kick, and the mother of the laddered-lisle was very upset indeed.

"Look, it was an accident—anyway, it just adds to her general schoolgirl . . . authenticity," said Ruby, pronouncing this big word with pride.

The mother didn't seem convinced, and the

schoolgirl twins were still getting all hot and bothered too, but then they were called into the audition room so they rushed off in a fluster.

"Us next," said Ruby. She took hold of me by the shoulders. "We're going to do great, Garnet. Better than any of this dopey stupid show-offy lot. You and me. Ruby and Garnet. We'll act it all out and it won't be scary at all, it'll just be like us playing in private at home. Trust me."

I tried. And then it was our turn. And it wasn't at all like playing in private. We were shown on to this stage and there were lots of people watching us and a camera filming us and I was so frightened I nearly fell over. Ruby grabbed me by the hand and said "Twin-grin" under her breath and marched us to the middle of the stage.

"Hi, twins," said this woman with short hair and a smock.

"Hi there," said Ruby, imitating her voice, trying to sound all cool and casual, though I could see little beads of sweat on her forehead.

She nudged me, and I squeaked "Hi" too.

"We've got our audition piece all prepared," Ruby said brightly, trying to show them we were dead professional. "I'm Pat and she's Isabel and I'm also Mam'zelle and at the end I'm Janet as well."

They all laughed, for some reason. I blushed, because I was scared they thought Ruby was silly, but Ruby didn't seem to mind. She laughed too.

"We'd love to see your little number sometime, twins, but right now we just want to test out your voices," said the woman with the short hair. "Sooo—twin number one. Tell me what you had to eat yesterday."

Ruby blinked at her. But then she threw back her hair, put her hand on one hip, and got started.

"Okay, you want to know what I had to eat yesterday. Well, breakfast was boring old granola again. Garnet and I used to have Coco Pops and jam sandwiches and they were yummy, but now we have this awful woman living with us, our dad's girlfriend, and she's into health foods so it's bye-bye Coco Pops, hello granola—all this oat and bran that makes your face ache munching and then there are these little raisins like rabbit droppings, yuck."

They were all laughing again, but this time even I could see that this was good. They loved Ruby.

"Right, now, twin two, tell us what you had for lunch," said the woman with short hair.

They stopped looking at Ruby. They looked at me. And Ruby looked at me too. Desperately. Terrified I was going to let us down.

I tried to pretend to myself that I wasn't shy stupid scaredy-cat Garnet. I made out I was Ruby. I threw back my hair. I put my hand on my hip. I opened my mouth to start.

I had it all worked out what I was going to do. I was going to tell about Rose's garlic pie and how it not only tasted absolutely disgusting, but people ducked and dodged for days afterward whenever we breathed in their direction and we'd worn out six toothbrushes already trying to take the taste away. I could be funny too if I really tried. I could be just as good as Ruby. I could.

But then someone came bursting through the door and stood there, staring. Dad!

And I couldn't. I simply couldn't.

He didn't say anything to stop me.

But he didn't need to. I couldn't get started, not in front of him. I opened my mouth—but nothing came out. I tried to speak, but I couldn't even squeak.

"Come on, *Garnet*," said Ruby.

I gulped, I opened my mouth, I tried. But all I managed was a goldfish impersonation.

"Look, I'll say what we had for lunch," said Ruby.

"No, sweetie, we've already heard you. We want your twin to talk now. Let's skip lunch. And snacks and supper. What time did you go to bed, twin two?"

I saw Ruby flash her eyes at me. I knew she was willing me to tell a funny story about our bed-delaying tactics, our constant unnecessary trips to the bathroom, our midnight raids on the fridge, our frequent nocturnal ramblings—all deliberately done to unnerve Dad and Rose, so that they could never totally relax into unwedded bliss.

I could tell it, but not in front of Dad.

So, after several centuries had gone by and I actually saw the short-haired woman glance at her watch, I started a stupid mumble about "Well, we're supposed to start getting ready for bed at nine, ten at weekends, but we often try to stay up."

My voice was this sad expressionless little squeak. I saw Ruby close her eyes in agony. I saw Dad hang his head. I saw the short-haired woman and all her colleagues shaking their heads. I saw it all and I shrank down to mouse-size to match my squeak.

"Thank you, sweetie. Off you go, twins. Next!"
said the short-haired woman. She was already
staring past us, smiling at the new set of twins.

"No, hang on a minute!" said Ruby. "Look my
sister isn't very well, she's been sick, she's not nor-
mally like this, she can speak up and be ever so
funny, I swear she can. How about if we just do
a couple of minutes of our prepared piece? Give
us a chance. We've used up all our savings getting
here, and we're going to get in terrible trouble
with our dad when we get back . . ."

"Yes, it's a shame, sweetie, but we don't really
have the time," said the short-haired woman, and
she put her arm around both of us. It wasn't just
sympathy. She propelled us gently but firmly to
the edge of the stage.

Even in the midst of her despair Ruby remembered the camera, twisting round and grimacing
in agony, and then she sighed and waved her
hand.

I could hear a few chuckles.

112

"That kid's a riot," said someone.

"Yeah. Pity about her twin."

It was only a murmur. But it was like a giant roaring in my ears. It wouldn't soften or stop.

I couldn't seem to hear properly even when Dad caught up with us.

"You bet you're in terrible trouble," he said furiously. "How dare you run off here like this, when I expressly forbade it. I couldn't believe it when we woke up and found you both gone. I was so worried I was going to call the police, but Rose insisted you'd both be all right and that you'd obviously gone for this idiotic audition."

"Well, it was a complete waste of time anyway," said Ruby. "You really blew it for us, Dad. We were doing just great and then you had to come barging in and put us off our timing."

"Put me off. Not you," I said. "And it wasn't Dad's fault. He waited. He gave us a chance. But I mucked it up. That's what they said. You were great, Ruby, yeah. But I was useless. They said so."

"No they didn't," said Ruby. "And anyway, they didn't give you a real chance. It wasn't fair."

"You don't want to be an actress anyway, Garnet," said Dad. "And even if you'd both been offered the parts, I wouldn't have let you take them. Ruby can act when she grows up, but I don't want my girls turning into ghastly little child stars, thank you very much."

113

"There's no chance of me being any sort of star," I said, and I started crying. I couldn't stand it. They were both so sorry for me. Dad was still mega-mad because we'd sneaked off to London by ourselves, but he was holding back his anger to try to comfort me.

And Ruby wasn't mad at me. She should hate me forever because I did mess it up. I should have said all that stuff, never mind about Dad being there. I could have done it. Only I didn't. I let her down. I'll always let her down.

She's the biggest and the brightest and the best.
She's the riot.
She's the star.
It's a pity she's stuck with me.
Pity about her twin.

Pity about her twin.

Pity about her twin.

What's all this pity piffle??? Puhlease, Garnet! And anyway, I did get mad at you. I chewed you out in the car, because you *were* a bit of a wimp at the audition. What did it matter if Dad was there or not? You could have made something up if you didn't want to rant on about Rose. I mean, I wouldn't go on about it if I really thought you couldn't do it, but you *can*. Well, you could have. Only it's too late now. We've blown it. Lost our chance. We don't get to be famous child stars. We're dull child nobodies stuck in this dreary dump forever and ever. *And* we've lost all our savings for nothing. Not to mention my baby doll that Gran gave me.

Garnet? Oh, don't start crying *again*.

Look, *I'm* the one who should be crying. *I'm* the one who wants to act. *I'm* the one that Dad is maddest at. The way he went on and on at me! And then when I argued back and told him he was an old worrywart and that we're big enough to look after ourselves and what possible harm could happen on a simple trip to London, I thought he was actually going to slug me.

He hasn't ever smacked us, has he? I wish he would, then we could show the bruises at school and get sent to a group home.

I mean it. I'm sick of living here with him and her.

Hey, let's write to Gran and see if she could possibly squeeze us into her place. We could sleep curled up on her couch, couldn't we? And she keeps sending postcards saying how much she misses us.

Then we could go back to our old school. We're not going to this stupid new school again, especially now that Dumbo Debenham's tattled on us. We're not going even if Dad picks us up and tries to drag us there. We're not speaking to him, right? And we're certainly not speaking to *Rose*. Who cares if she came out with all that stuff about us being ultradetermined and clever getting ourselves to London. We didn't ask her to stick up for us, did we?

Garnet? Look, what does it matter what she's shouting? We don't want to go and watch television with her! Who cares if it's—

It was us! Well, only a glimpse, but they showed me, doing my good-bye bit. The camera came right up close. They didn't show much of

Garnet, just a bit of her hair and an elbow but
they showed all of me, and there was a voice-
over saying, "And this twin certainly took rejec-
tion like a trouper."

Too bad they didn't say our names. Still. We
were on television. Well, I was.

It was on the news. We missed the first part
but Rose videotaped it. They did a whole feature
about the audition for the Twins at St. Clare's
series as an early promo for the program, seeing
that it's going to be made by the same television
company. They showed some of those other
twins doing their party pieces. There weren't

any as good as us. Well, me. Of course, that's only my opinion.

The twins that they've chosen are absolutely *awful*.

That's the way they talk, too. Ooh, absolutely jolly good show, fwightfully, ya, jolly super-duper green-welly wallies.

Perhaps it's just as well we weren't chosen. If they'd got us to talk all twiddly-snooty-pop like that then we'd never have heard the end of it. Kids won't watch a pathetic program like that. Or if they do, they'll just laugh at it.

Still, it looks like they're going all out on the production. It's being filmed on location in this real big boarding school during the summer vacation. They showed all the grounds. It was just like some millionaire's mansion. And there was a swimming pool. And a sort of miniature zoo, where they keep their pets. And inside this huge great house it wasn't a bit like a *school* school. There were ordinary boring old classrooms but they had playrooms with television and videos and music centers and computers and upstairs there weren't dormitories like I thought—they had lots of bedrooms with flowery comforters and teddies on the beds and posters up on the walls, and best of all, this school has its own *theater*. It's quite small, but it's got a real stage with red velvet curtains and lighting and props and everything, and they put on plays.

I wish we could go to a school like that.

Hey.

Wow.

Yes!

No!

Oh, Garnet, come on! It would be absolutely fantastic! Oh, let's go there. We wouldn't be acting, we'd be the *real* twins of St. Clare's. Well, Marnock Heights. It would be such fun. We could play all those fancy games—field hockey and lacrosse and softball in the summer. I bet I'd be absolutely ace at softball. And we could each have a pet in the little zoo place. Twin pets.

Rabbits? Those little ones with shy faces. Dwarf rabbits.

Okay, twin baby bunnies. Though I'd rather have gerbils. Or rats.

I don't like rats. Or gerbils. I don't even like mice.

Right, we're agreed. It's rabbits. We'll go and play with our rabbits every day and we'll have a game of softball and we'll swim in the pool and in the evenings we'll watch videos in the lounge and then, after we've gone to bed, we'll have mega-midnight feasts.

This is a game, isn't it?

No! It can be real. We're going to go to boarding school.

Yes, it's a school, so there'll be lessons all day. We can't just mess around petting our rabbits and playing games. There'll be English and History and Technology. And hard stuff too like Geometry and Latin.

That's okay. You'll be able to do that. And did you see that library in the film clip? All those wonderful books, Garnet.

We've got books here.

Old boring books. We hate this bookshop. We hate this school and this whole horrible dump of a village. So we're going to get out. We're going to go to boarding school. Marnock Heights. We'll write a letter applying. You'd better do it, Garnet, your writing's much neater than mine. I'll tell you what to put.

But I don't want to—

I'm sick of you going on about what you want and don't want. Look, *I* wanted to be one of the twins of St. Clare's on television. *I* planned and plotted so that we got all the way to London by ourselves. *I* sold all my stuff. *I* did my audition thing so well that they all laughed and they really liked me, and it looked like we'd actually got the part, didn't it? But then *you* messed it up.

Yes.

There's no need to look like that. I'm not being deliberately mean. I'm just trying to get you to understand that it would be ultra ultra ultra mean of you to mess up my chances of getting what I want second best in the world. Right?

The Red Bookshop
High Street
Cussop
19 May

Dear Madam—We are sorry, we don't know your name.

We are ten-year-old identical twins, nearly eleven and we hate our school in this village. We don't fit in. The classes are boring and there aren't any good books and the only game we play is soccer.

We went to the television audition for _The Twins at St. Clare's_. We very nearly got the part. We were featured in the television coverage. Well, one of us was. And you were featured too and your wonderful school and we thought Ooh this is our idea of heaven, the stage and the swimming pool and the games and the animals and all that.

So please can we come to your school in September? We promise to be good pupils and you don't have to worry about us being homesick because we hate our home.
Yours faithfully,

Ruby Barker

Garnet Barker

P.S. Please say yes. You won't be sorry. Really.

Look at this!

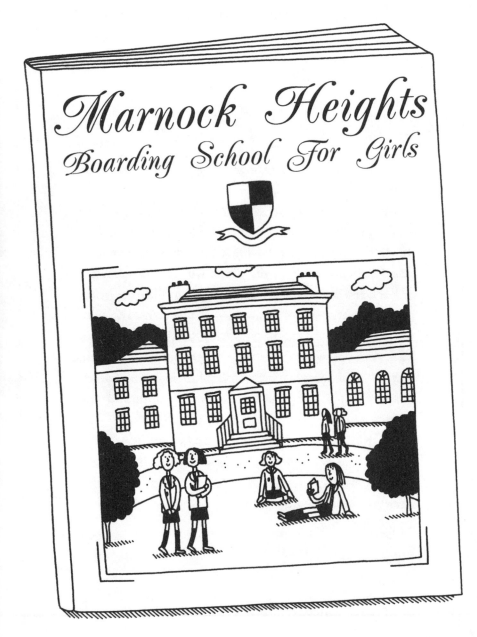

We went rushing to tell Dad. We thought he'd be in a good mood because some nutty old girl had bought all his *Girls' Own* magazine annuals for a lot of money, and as she staggered backward and forward to her car with book after book she kept burbling, "Those were the days, eh? When girls really *were* girls. A hard game of field hockey and then toasted muffins in front of the fire." She sighed happily, and then saw Garnet and me hanging around.

"Only nowadays it's all disco dancing and McDonald's hamburgers," she said. "That's what you want, isn't it, girls?"

"Oh no," I said quickly. "Garnet and me, we'd like to play hockey and toast muffins. That's just what we want too."

"Well, good for you," said the old girl, lurching out of the shop with the last of her annuals.

"What's all this about?" said Dad, blinking at us. But he looked pleased. We've had a policy of being rude to the customers recently and that's made him really mad. I looked at Garnet. She looked at me. I took a deep breath.

"We're not kidding, Dad. We read all the St. Clare's books, see, when we were wanting to act in the TV series. And we think it all sounds really great. So Garnet and I want to go to boarding school."

Dad laughed, not taking us seriously.

"It's not really like it is in books," said Dad. "I don't think either of you would be thrilled at a real boarding school. You have to work hard and do as you're told all the time. According to poor Miss Debenham, you don't do any work at all and never do as you're told."

"Yes, but that's because she's a silly teacher and it's a silly school. But if we went to a super top-notch boarding school then we'd be megagood, really and truly. A boarding school like Marnock Heights."

"Like *where?*"

"It's the place they're using for the St. Clare's film. It's a real school. And so Garnet and I wrote to the principal asking to go there and she's sent us this booklet all about it. Look."

I ran to get it and shoved it under Dad's nose.

"Oh, for goodness' sake! Will you girls *stop* doing things behind my back," Dad groaned.

"Say we can go, though, Dad, *please*. You can look at all the pictures. It's lovely, isn't it?"

"Oh, very lovely," said Dad, flipping through. Then he stopped at the back page, where there were two pieces of paper tucked into a little pocket. "And very lovely tuition fees too! Twelve thousand a year. Each! Oh yes, nice one, Ruby."

I stared at him and then snatched the paper. There were all these numbers on it. The tuition. I didn't realize you had to *pay* to go to some schools. You had to pay an enormous enormous enormous amount to go to Marnock Heights.

"Oh no," I wailed.

"Oh no," Garnet wailed too. But she didn't sound too upset, actually. Right, Garnet??

Well...

We've got to think POSITIVE. Because all is not lost. Maybe Dad won't have to fork out any money. Not that he could anyway. We're far too poor. But But But . . . There was a letter tucked into the pocket of the booklet, along with the note about the terrible tuition.

Marnock Heights
Gorselea
Sussex
22 May

Dear Ruby and Garnet,

What lovely names! You wrote me a lovely letter too. I'm pleased that you'd like to attend Marnock Heights. Here is the current prospectus. Show it to your parents or guardians.

I'd like to point out that we do award several special scholarships each year. These have already been awarded for the autumn, but one girl is now unable to accept her scholarship because she's going abroad. Perhaps you would like to come to the school and take the entrance examination to see if either of you might pass highly enough for scholarship consideration?

Please telephone my secretary for an appointment.

With best wishes,

Yours sincerely,
Miss Jeffreys
Principal
(There, you know my name now!)

Chapter 11

Dad still wouldn't consider it. At first. But we kept on at him.

You *kept on at him.*

On and on and on. And then he started to weaken.

It was Rose too. She said we should try for it. She said she wished she'd had a decent education.
"It's a great chance. It's a very famous school. If one of them got a scholarship there then they'd be able to go on, do anything, achieve anything."

She's just desperate to get rid of us. Because we're driving her crackers.

You sometimes drive me crackers, Ruby. You won't ever change your mind about anyone.

Or anything. So we're going to Marnock Heights!

We're taking the exam, that's all. And I don't see the point, because there's two of us and only one scholarship.

We'll wangle two, somehow. Once Miss Jeffreys gets to know us. She likes us already. She's very complimentary in her letter. We're lovely. I'm Miss Lovely Ruby and you're Miss Lovely Garnet, okay? Oh, come *on*, Garnet, cheer up! We've won! We've got our own way!

You've got your own way. And I'm worried about the exam. She doesn't say what sort of exam it is. If it's an interview then I'm scared I'll get all stupid and shy and not know what to say. Like at the audition.

It's okay, I'll do all the talking. You just leave it to me.

So I left the talking to Ruby. We were shown

130

into Miss Jeffreys' study and she shook our hands
and smiled and gave us tea and cookies and as we
sipped and nibbled, Miss Jeffreys asked us questions.

They were really hard questions too, like:
"Why do you think education for girls is important?"

and "What are your ambitions for the future?"

and "What do you like doing in your spare
time?"

and even "How do you feel about being a
twin?"

I feel bad about being a twin because I let Ruby
down. I couldn't think of a thing to say. I just
tagged on to the end of her sentences. She was
brilliant.

Hmm! *Mega*-brilliant.

It was a cinch. I didn't say what I *really* think, naturally. I just said all this stuff to impress Miss Jeffreys and make her see that we are ideal pupils for Marnock Heights. I don't care a bit about education but I spouted stuff that old Rosy-Ratbag said the other day. And I said, truthfully enough, that our ambition is to be famous actresses, but I said we needed to study Shakespeare and if we stay in Cussop you don't even get *started* on Shakespeare until you're a senior. And I said that in our spare time we acted, and we also read a lot, and I named all the books that Garnet likes, and some of Dad's Dickens and Hardy, and Miss Jeffreys looked impressed. She asked about the stories but I made some stuff up and I'm sure she swallowed it. And then when she asked about the twin business I said it was just like being one person, only we were twice as good as anyone else.

She laughed and said that was a really good answer.

So *I* said that it was ever so important that we must never be separated and that since we always shared everything maybe we could share a scholarship too.

Dad got all fidgety then but she laughed even more. Then she took us all around the school and the grounds, and it is truly fantastic.

The other girls seem okay too. One looked a little snobbish so I stuck my tongue out at her, but she stuck her tongue out back at me and then we both grinned. She had red hair and little wicked eyes. I think we'll be friends with her when we come to Marnock Heights.

If.

Look, I keep *telling* you, Garnet, we'll get there. Okay, we had to sit in the library and do that boring old written exam—and I must admit that got me a bit worried because that other teacher insisted that we sit at opposite ends so we couldn't work together the way we always do. That was unfair. And then, when I caught your eye and we were sort of conferring, it was mean of that teacher to make me turn around and face the other way. They don't understand. We weren't cheating or anything. It's just the way we work, isn't it? Especially when it comes to all that boring stuff like arithmetic and general knowledge. And that composition was ultra-blobby-boring. "Snow in Winter"! What did you write, eh?

You'll get mad at me.

Oh no. What did you put???

I just imagined a mountain covered all over with snow and what it must look like. And how odd it must be for the sheep, all green grass one minute and then white sharp stuff that hurts their teeth. And people always say there's a blanket of snow on the ground and yet if you were under that blanket, buried, you'd be dead. And how once when we were making snow angels in the park I stopped moving my arms and legs to see what it would feel like to be frozen. And snow looks so clean and pure but nothing's dirtier when everyone's trudged through it and it's all gray with yellow patches. I wrote how it's always like that, snow can't ever stay fresh and new, and yet each time you hope there'll be a way of keeping it looking beautiful.

Oh yucky yucky yuck! What did you have to write that garbage for? I just scribbled down a few things about robins and icicles and footsteps crunching, like the verses inside Christmas cards. That's what they wanted, you idiot, not all your weirdo rambling.

I'm sorry, Ruby.

Yes, well, you should be.

Ruby . . . What if you get accepted for the scholarship and I don't?

We're *both* going to get a scholarship.

But what if we don't? Would you go to Marnock Heights without me?

I keep telling and telling you, we're going together.

Yes, and I keep asking and asking . . . if it's just you that gets accepted, will you go?

No. Yes. I don't *know.*

I think you should. Though it would be horrible without you. But I can't stand it if I'm always going to be the one that holds you back.

We're not going to be held back, either of us. We're going rushing forward. To Marnock Heights.

Marnock Heights
Gorselea
Sussex
29 May

Dear Mr. Barker,

I thoroughly enjoyed meeting you and your delightful daughters last week.

Ruby is a charming child, so full of vim and vigor. No wonder she wants to be an actress. I am sure she will succeed in her ambitions one day. I'm afraid we can't offer her a scholarship at Marnock Heights. She is obviously witty and intelligent and her conversation sparkles—though she tends to get rather carried away and bluffs when she's uncertain! Her written work is lively if a little slapdash, but I'm afraid she failed several of our tests. If she could only apply herself more vigorously then I'm sure she could reach a far higher standard. I feel she's relied on her sister to do all her work for so long that she's failed to reach her full academic potential.

Garnet too might benefit from a term of separation from her sister. She lets Ruby do all her talking for her and therefore does not interview at all well. However, she came into her own in the written tests. She has a few gaps in her knowledge but on the whole she did very well. Her essay was outstanding—extremely sensitive and mature. We would like to offer her a full scholarship at Marnock Heights, beginning with the autumn term.

With best wishes,

Yours sincerely,
Miss Jeffreys
Principal

*We couldn't believe it. We thought Miss Jeffreys
got us mixed up.*

*"She means me," said Ruby. "She must mean
me."*

*"Yes, it can't be me," I said. "Ruby must have
gotten the scholarship."*

"No," said Dad. "It's definitely Garnet."

"Let me see the letter!" Ruby demanded.

Dad didn't want either of us to see it.

*"It's addressed to me," he said. "And it's plain
what it says. There's no mix-up."*

*"She's just got our names the wrong way
around," Ruby insisted. "It's always happening."*

"Not this time," said Rose.

*"Look, it's absolutely not fair if Rose has read
the letter too, when it's got nothing to do with her.
She's not our mother," said Ruby.*

*"No, but I'm your father, and I want you to
calm down, Ruby, and we'll talk all this over carefully."*

"Not till you show me the letter!"

"I'd show both the girls the letter," said Rose. "They're not little kids. I think they should see what it says."

So Dad showed us.

It was like a smack in the face.

Not for me. For Ruby.

I read faster than she does. I watched her face while she was finishing the letter. I couldn't take it.

"She's written a whole load of garbage," I said quickly. "She only met us for one afternoon and yet she thinks she knows us. Well she doesn't, does she, Ruby?"

Ruby was getting very red in the face. She screwed up her eyes. She looked as if she was trying hard not to cry. But Ruby never cries.

"Ruby," I said, and I put my arm around her.

She wriggled away as if my arm had turned into a snake.

"Oh, Ruby," I said, and I was the one who started crying. "Look, I'm not going to go to Marnock Heights. I didn't want to go in the first place. It was you that wanted to, not me."

I was making it worse.

"I think you should go, Garnet," said Rose. "You've done very well. We should all be congratulating you. I know it's tough on Ruby, but—"

"You don't know anything," I shouted.

I couldn't stand it. I didn't want them ganging up on my side. I was on Ruby's side.

"Hey, we'll have less of that sassy tone," said Dad. "Rose, dear, could you make us all a cup of cocoa? Let's talk it over, eh? It's been a bit of a shock for all of us. Ruby? Ruby, where are you going?"

"There's nothing to talk about," said Ruby. Her voice sounded awful. She was trying to make it sound couldn't-care-less, but it kept catching in her throat. "Garnet's got the scholarship. I haven't. And that's it."

"But I'm not going, Ruby! Please believe me. I promise I'm not going to go. I couldn't stand going there. Especially without you."

"So why did you try so hard on all those silly tests and write all that yucky stuff for your essay?" said Ruby.

141

"I don't know. I just didn't think. Oh, Ruby, I'm sorry."

I tried to grab hold of her again but she wouldn't let me.

"Get away from me," she said, ducking.

"Now this is getting ridiculous," said Dad. "Pull yourself together, Ruby. I'm ashamed of you. I know you're very disappointed, but there's no need to be nasty to poor old Garnet. Why can't you be big enough to congratulate her? She didn't act like this over that television audition, now did she? She was full of praise for you."

Dad was making it worse. I saw Ruby's eyes, as she ducked. They were brimming over.

"Oh, congratulations, clever goody-goody Garnet," Ruby gabbled, and then she rushed out the room.

I tried to follow her, but Dad stopped me.

"No, Garnet. Let her go. She won't want you around for a while, especially since she's crying," he said. Perhaps he did understand a little after all. "But there's no need for you to cry, sweetheart. Rose is right. You've done brilliantly and I'm very proud of you."

"I'm not going, though," I wept.

"Well. I can't make you go. And this boarding school business certainly wasn't my idea. But I think now that it's a wonderful opportunity."

"I'll say," said Rose, handing around the cocoa. "You've got to go for it, Garnet."

"I can't leave Ruby," I wailed.

"But Ruby would leave you," said Rose.

"That's different," I said.

"But it shouldn't be different," said Dad, and he pulled me onto his lap. "This letter has made me see that maybe it's bad for you and Ruby to be together all the time. You're holding each other back, spoiling each other's chances. You're growing up now, and you need to develop as two separate sisters."

"But we're not separate. We're twins. We can't do without each other."

"You're going to have to learn to some day," said Dad. "You'll both grow up and have different jobs and have different lifestyles and have different families."

"No, we're going to stay together," I said.

We'd got it all figured out.

We'd stick together when we were young

and when we were old

and when we were even older

*and if we ever wanted to get married then we'd
marry twins*

and have twin babies

and then when they grew up they *could stick together forever and maybe they'd have twins too and then* they *could . . .*
My head was buzzing with all these twins. I wanted my own twin. I could hear her upstairs. She was sobbing.

I don't know what to do.
It's worse than when Ruby wasn't talking to me.
She's talking now, but not really. *And she only talks when we're with other people. When we're together she hardly says anything. She won't play any of our games. She won't plan any twin-tricks so that we do things simultaneously.*
She doesn't seem to want to be a twin anymore.
She won't even dress like me now. She waits until she sees what I'm putting on and then she puts on something entirely different. And she does her hair in a new way too.

I tried to copy her, so she changed it again.

And so I changed too. And then she did something terrible. She got the scissors and I thought she was bluffing. And then I wasn't sure.

"Don't!" I said.

But she did. She cut off all her hair.

"Oh, Ruby, what have you done?*" I said, looking at her poor head with the chopped hair sticking up like a scrubbing brush.*

"I'm making me different," she said, running

146

her hand through the stubble. She swallowed and sniffed. "And you needn't look like that. I like it. I wanted it this way for ages. It's . . . sort of punk. Great."

I didn't know what to do. We've always had long hair, right from when we were little. When Gran made us have braids I would always do Ruby's as well as my own. Sometimes when I was feeling sleepy I'd forget which was my head and which was hers.

Now when I stared at Ruby I felt as if my own hair had been hacked off even though I could still feel the warm weight of it on my shoulders. It gave me the weirdest out-of-sync feeling, like when you watch a film and the people say things a fraction before their lips open.

Ruby couldn't grow her hair. So there was only one thing to do.

"No you don't!" Ruby snapped as I reached for

the scissors. She snatched them away from me.
"I'm warning you, Garnet. You cut off your hair
and I'll cut off your head!"

She looked so fierce that I believed her.

She looked like she hated me.

She took the scissors and some newspaper and
cut out a line of paper dolls. She cut them into
twins. And then she chopped through their
hands, so they were separate.

She chopped so violently that they tore all the
way up their arms.

It's me again. Ruby won't write in the book anymore. I don't want to write much either. How can
I give an account of us when we aren't us anymore?

If only I could tear out all the pages about the

school and the scholarship—scrub them out so that they never happened.

Ruby's acting like she wants to scrub me out completely. It's vacation time now, but she won't hang around with me. She just goes off by herself and when I try to follow her she runs away. She could always run faster than me. And she's better at hiding. I don't know where she goes or whether she joins up with anyone else. But she won't join up with me.

I asked her in bed at night if we could go back to being us if I wrote a letter to Miss Jeffreys saying I wasn't going to Marnock Heights.

I waited. The room was very dark but I could see her eyes open, watching me. She waited too.

Then she said into the silence, "I don't care if you go or not, Garnet. You do what you like. And I'll do what I like. But we're not us anymore and we can't ever be. We'll still be split up even if we stay together."

But it's not what I like. I don't know what I like.

I don't want to go to Marnock Heights. Although I've been reading all these books. Not the twins ones. I feel sick whenever I see them. No, there's a whole shelf of old school stories at the back of the shop—girls who go to schools in Abbeys and Chalets and Towers—and I've been reading one in the morning and one in the after-

*noon and sometimes one in the evening too and
sometimes—just sometimes—it sounds as if it
might be fun.*

*Judy thinks so. She's jealous. She comes
around to the shop sometimes. I've been to her
house. She's got all these tapes and videos. You
just have to sit and watch and listen. Or we go up
to her bedroom and play games. Not our sort of
games. Board games. And I do get a bit bored
playing them. Judy's okay but she's a bit boring
too.*

*She says she's seen Ruby going around with
Jeremy Treadgold and his gang! Ruby with the
Giant Blob? I asked Ruby but she just rubbed the
end of her nose, indicating that I should mind my
own business.*

*Ruby doesn't want to be my business anymore.
She's made herself different.
She even looks different.*

People maybe wouldn't even think we were twins now.

Gran nearly blew her top when she came to stay for the weekend. This old man, Albert, drove her in his car. He's her neighbor in her apartment building. He came and stayed too, which made it a bit of a squeeze. Gran said we should call him Uncle Albert, though he's not our uncle.

I looked at Ruby and she looked at me and just for a second it was almost like the old days.

But these are new days and everything's changing and Ruby's changed most of all.

"Whatever *have* you done to yourself, Ruby?" Gran demanded. "What do you look like? You're so scruffy. Like a gutter child. And your HAIR! Oh my Lord, have you got lice?"

"Leave me alone, Gran," said Ruby, fidgeting and scowling.

"For goodness' sake, how could you let her run around like a ragamuffin?" Gran said to Rose.

Rose had tried to fix Ruby up a little for Gran's visit. She'd washed all her best clothes and ironed them and she'd begged Ruby to let her try to neaten up her new hairstyle. Ruby refused. She wore her oldest dirtiest clothes and deliberately fished her old wornout sneakers out of the trash, even though Rose had bought her brand-new ones specially.

But Rose didn't say any of this.

"Ruby likes to be comfortable. And we think her hairstyle really suits her, don't we, Ricky?"

"Sure," said Dad, putting his arm around Rose.

"Well, at least Garnet looks fairly presentable,"

Gran sniffed. "But what's all this I hear about you being packed off to boarding school, Garnet? I don't hold with that idea at all. What's the matter, do they want to get rid of you?"

"Of course we don't want to get rid of her!" said Dad. "We just think she should give it a try for a term, seeing that she's got this scholarship. But if she hates it then of course she can come home whenever she wants."

But like I said, I still don't know what I want. I'm starting to get nightmares about going to the school.

And yet it's horrible at home now that Ruby is a stranger instead of a sister. I'd hoped that I could talk to Gran in secret and ask her if I could maybe go and live with her for a while—but I'd forgotten how naggy and picky she can be sometimes. And then there's Albert who isn't our uncle. He's not part of our family but it looks as if he and Gran are a new family all of their own.

Then there's Dad and Rose. They have fights sometimes but they always make up. Once when Rose did her best to cook a real Sunday lunch for everyone, somehow the beef got burned and the popovers were flat and the potatoes wouldn't roast and the beans went stringy and the gravy had lumps. Dad still ate up every scrap on his plate and said it was super and even asked for seconds.

They're a family too.

I'm part of their family and Gran's family and I used to have Mom as a special family but even more than Mom there was always Ruby.
Ruby-and-Garnet.
Only now there's just Ruby. And Garnet.

Ruby?

Ruby.

Oh, Ruby.

Chapter 13

This is my written work. And I don't care if it's slapdash. Who cares what that stupid jumped-up jelly-belly Jeffreys says?

I wouldn't want to go there anyway. Not now. I'm having heaps more fun here. I am.

Anyway, I bet Garnet doesn't have the guts to go without me.

Or if she does, I bet she gets terribly homesick and cries buckets and will be sent back a soggy wreck.

She can't manage without me. Even she knows that.

But I'm doing just fine without her.

This is my new notebook and I shall take heaps of notes. It says MEMORANDUM on the cover. I like the first two letters. ME ME ME ME ME ME ME ME ME ME ME ME ME ME ME ME ME.

This notebook is going to be all about Me.

I like being just me.

I like it just me. Oh, I've put that part before. Never mind. It makes it twice as true. I feel GREAT.

I know what Memorandum means, too. I am really quite intelligent, even if some people seem to think I'm a total blockhead. "Memorandum" means notes of things to be remembered. And I want it officially down on paper that
1. Ruby Barker doesn't give two hoots about not getting that stupid scholarship.

2. Ruby Barker doesn't give two hoots that her sneaky sister is going instead of her.

3. Ruby Barker doesn't give two hoots about her sneaky sister.

She is *absolutely devastated* (there, *I'm* the one who uses such fancy long grown-up words, so it just goes to show that Miss Jeffreys is talking GARBAGE).

Yuck! Now. Where was I?

Oh yes. Garnet is truly despairing because I have broken up our twinship. She needs me. She may think she's the clever one now, but she's wrong! She's utterly lost without me. But *I'm* fine. I don't need her. Not one *bit* of her.

Well, maybe her fingers would come in handy some of the time. So she could do the writing when I get bored.

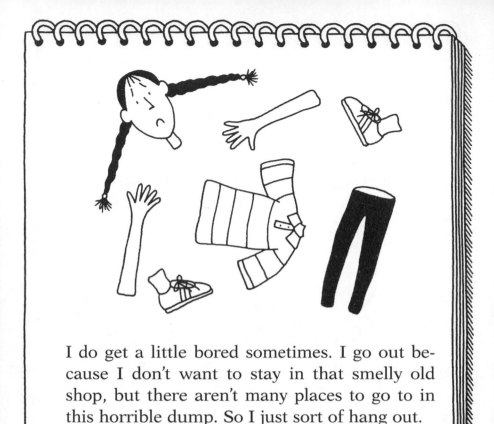

I do get a little bored sometimes. I go out because I don't want to stay in that smelly old
shop, but there aren't many places to go to in
this horrible dump. So I just sort of hang out.

I don't need Garnet to make up games for me.
I can make up my own. I mostly pretend I'm
this intrepid explorer trekking through
the jungle, and there are killer
snakes and huge hairy poi-
sonous spiders

and ferocious tigers

and I wade through the rapids

and hang by my fingertips from dangerous mountains

and whenever I get the slightest glimpse of the enemy I have to hide because in spite of my superhuman powers and mega-brilliance I am hopelessly outnumbered.

I am planning an ambush when I catch the Blob by himself.

The Intrepid Explorer often starves for days and days. She has to make quick raids into enemy territory

but often has to make do with natural resources.

The Intrepid Explorer did ponder about doing a bit of hunting

but she decided she was a vegetarian. Even though she isn't particularly crazy about vegetables. Sprouts . . . yuck. Cabbage . . . yuck. Cauliflower . . . double yuck.

If this is a *Memorandum* book, then it's just about *me* . . . and I can jot things down at *random*. I know what that means too, Miss Jeffreys, so nyah nyah to you too. It means there's no plan, and you just shove things in any old how. So these are my random jottings.

I am Ruby Barker and I am a brilliant actress and if my ex-twin hadn't made such a mess of things then I could be starring in a TV series this summer.

I tried phoning the television people, telling them I was willing to audition for any other part. They thanked me and said they'd get in touch. But they didn't. So I phoned again and they got a bit snappish this time and said there weren't any parts available, sorry and all that but would I quit pestering them please, and if I really wanted to be an actress I needed to get myself an agent and why didn't I go to a good stage school.

Well, how can I go to a good stage school when my rotten old father won't send me to one, though he's sending my sister to the fanciest boarding school in the country?

Okay, he doesn't have to pay tuition, but her uniform is costing a *fortune*.

You should see it too. Talk about awful and old-fashioned! I wouldn't be caught *dead* in those clothes. Garnet looks *appalling*.

165

Well, I suppose Dad isn't having to pay out of his own pocket. Rose helped Garnet sell her doll at an auction. The crummy china baby doll, twin to mine. I sold mine at the flea market and they gave me $30.

It is exceedingly painful to have to write this next part. Garnet's doll went for $900. Yes. Mine would have been worth that too. It's some rare French make and daffy doll collectors are willing to fork out a fortune. I mean, you could probably buy a real baby for that kind of money.

Rose was very very angry when she found out the flea market people only gave me $30. Not angry with me, with them. She went and found them and made a great fuss, but they argued that it had been a perfectly fair deal and she was in the business and she should know they weren't running a kiddie's charity. But they did very reluctantly hand over $150. As a gesture. Rose was still cross because she said they must have made heaps more, but I was happy because that $150 is mine, and although boring old Dad said I should put it in a savings account, Rose said she didn't see why I shouldn't have some spending money since I was having a tough time just lately.

Only I'm not having a tough time at all. Like I said, I'm fine. Doing great. Couldn't be better.

And I've ended up with $75 to spend all on ME (plus $75 in Dad's boring old savings and loan).

I don't have to waste it on a horrible, hideous school uniform either. And special suitcases and hockey sticks and dressing gowns and frightful Clarks clodhopper shoes.

I can spend it on

or

or

or

or

or

or

It's weird. I've never had my very own money to spend before. I've always had to share. So it's great to get twice as much.

It's just that I can't quite get used to being just me.

I don't even look like me. It's a shock whenever I see myself in the mirror. My hair's growing a little but it seems to have lost all idea of gravity. It's growing *up*.

This has attracted comments from certain uncouth local loonies, inquiring whether I'm a boy or a girl.

I soon took care of them.

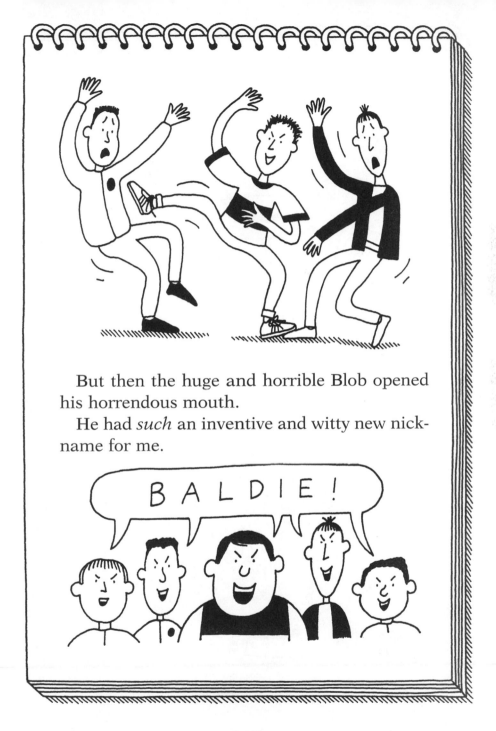

But then the huge and horrible Blob opened his horrendous mouth.

He had *such* an inventive and witty new nickname for me.

So I invented several new names for him and his stupid buddies.

So then they got all these grass clippings and asked me if I'd like a green wig and then they threw them all over me

so I hid behind a bush until I heard them coming and then I jumped up and yelled that they
all talked a lot of garbage so look out—
and they got this black plastic bag full of
garbage all over them.

I'd just grabbed a bag out of someone's
garbage can. I hadn't looked inside. It turned
out it was wondrously smelly soggy stuff, all
sour milk and coffee grounds and half-eaten
Chinese takeout . . .

So then they got really mad and yelled, "Let's
get her!"

I didn't run away quite fast enough.

So they got me.

And they smeared garbage on me and I hit them and they kicked me and I bit them but there was only one of me and there were a lot of them.

And then while Blob and I were swinging away at each other, this horrible boy with ferret teeth got his arm around my neck and started choking me and I tried to reach around and hit him where it really hurts but he was hurting that wobbly thing where you swallow so much that I couldn't move and Ferret-Face yelled, "Go on then, Jerry, bash her face in!" and I thought, This is it. I've already lost my hair. Now I'm going to lose my looks. I'm going to have to go around with a broken nose and no teeth for the rest of my days, and it's not going to help my acting career one bit, and I had my face all squeezed up ready for the blow but Blob hesitated.

"Let go of her, Brian, she's choking," he said.

"Well, hit her then!"

"Not with you hanging on to her. And all you others. It's not fair. We'll just fight it out, her and me."

Ferret-Face muttered and moaned, but he did let go. I staggered a bit, rubbing my sore neck.

"Are you okay?" said Blob.

"'Course I am," I croaked.

"Right. Let's fight," said Blob.

So he gave me a punch on the shoulder. Quite a soft punch. And I gave him a shove in his stomach. But not too hard. And then he wrestled me to the ground. But carefully. And I kicked at him. Though I barely touched him. We seemed to have lost interest in a really ferocious fight. We were just sort of going through the motions.

Ferret-Face and the other guys got bored with the whole situation too. And they were fed up being covered in all the stinky guck from the garbage bag, so they slunk off home.

Blob and I were left.

"Shall we just say that I've won the fight and call it quits?" said Blob.

"You haven't won the rotten fight!" I said indignantly. I gave him another punch, though it was a very feeble one.

"All right, all right. Well, how about if we call it a draw?" said Blob.

I thought a while. And then I nodded.

"Okay. Though I could have won, you know," I insisted.

"You're quite a good fighter. For a girl," said Blob.

"You're quite a good fighter. For a big fat blob," I said.

He looked hurt. "Hey, there's no need to call me names. I stuck up for you! I stopped Brian from mangling your neck."

"Yes, but you call me names. Baldie."

"Yes, well, you do look sort of bald since you got that wacky haircut."

"Yes, well, you do look a bit blobby."

"We *both* look a sight. Especially now. Covered in all this gunk," said Blob, wiping bamboo shoots out of his eye.

"You can say that again," I agreed, picking coffee grounds off my face.

We looked at each other. Then we laughed.

And it's weird. We're not bitter enemies anymore. We're sort of friends.

I sometimes go around in the gang, though I can't stand Brian. Actually, Blob doesn't like him very much either.

So we've started going around together. Just him and me.

He still calls me Baldie.

I still call him Blob.

But it doesn't matter because we're pals.

It's great to have someone to pal around with. Someone different, not someone the same as me.

And both Blob and I are going on to the big

school together. I'm glad I'll be rid of that Dumbo Debenham. I'll be a new girl at a new school with new teachers. I could make a whole new start if I wanted to. Work a little.

Well, that's what Dad says.

I'll have to see about that.

But there is one good thing about the new school. They've got a stage. Not quite as fancy and elaborate as the one at Marnock Heights, but they've got velvet curtains, and they can put up special lights and rustle up some scenery and they have a real play in the summer and a pageant at Christmas. Blob told me, because his sister's been in them.

So I'm going to get to be in them too.

Definitely.

It's all going to be great.

I'm ever so happy.

Garnet isn't happy. She's started crying at night. She's scared about going to boarding school by herself. But it's not just that. She says she can't bear not being friends with me anymore.

I listen. And sometimes my eyes sting a bit, but it's okay in the dark. She can't see.

I open my mouth to say a whole lot of things. But somehow I can't get them said into the silence. I can't even manage one word. Sorry.

Well, I don't see why I should say sorry. It's Garnet's fault she's going. She shouldn't have done so well in that stupid entrance exam.

No, she should have tried harder at the audition. Then we'd have got to be the Twins at St. Clare's. We'd be acting now. Together.

We've been separate all summer.

It's been a bit strange sometimes.

It's going to be even stranger when she's gone.

It's her last night at home. Rose cooked fried

potatoes and chicken, Garnet's favorite, and
made a cake.

She's never made *me* a special cake.
Garnet could only manage one small slice.
Then we all had to sit around playing stupid
games like Snap and Happy Families. Pretending we were all one Happy Family. And Garnet
looked like she was going to Snap.

But she didn't cry. Not even when we went to bed. At least, I don't think she did. I got right under the covers so that I couldn't hear.

I felt as if I were snapping. In half.

I kept pretending it wasn't really happening but then we woke up in the morning and Garnet got dressed in her strange new uniform and we've never looked less like twins in our lives.

Rose came into our bedroom to help Garnet get all her new stuff packed and ready.

I looked at all the new clothes and the pajamas and the field hockey boots and all the other stuff, all exactly my size. But not for me.

And for the first time I was really glad I wasn't going. I knew I'd be scared.

Garnet was so scared she had an upset stomach and had to keep dashing to the bathroom. One of the times she was off in the bathroom I picked up her old nightie lying on her pillow and sort of snuggled into it for a second, like a baby with a security blanket.

Rose was bent over Garnet's suitcase but she turned and saw me.

She didn't say anything—but she straightened up and put her arm around me and gave me a quick hug.

I started to wriggle away, but she held on to me. So I found I was kind of hugging her back.

And then I started crying.

"You're the one who never cries. You'll start me off," Rose whispered.

"Don't be nice to me. I've been so hateful. To Garnet," I sobbed.

"You haven't been exactly sweetness and light to me, either," said Rose, laughing shakily. "Or your dad. But you're right. It's Garnet that really matters."

It's Garnet that really matters.

My twin. My best friend. My other half.

She came back from the bathroom and I rushed at her, flinging my arms around her neck.

"Oh, Garnet, I'm so sorry, I've been such a pig,

I didn't mean it really, I was just so jealous, and I felt so stupid, and I felt so left out, but you will still be my twin, won't you, even though you're off to Marnock Heights?"

"I'll be your twin forever and ever and ever,"

said Garnet, and we hugged so hard we seemed like Siamese twins, joined forever.

Only we were about to be ripped apart.

"It's all my stupid stupid stupid fault," I wailed. "Oh Garnet, I'll miss you so terribly."

"I'll miss you too, Ruby—ever so ever so much. But Dad says I don't have to stay if I really hate it."

"And you'll come home some weekends—and all the breaks. Oh, how can I have been crazy enough to waste all this summer being so rotten? I hate me. Why do I always have to be the bad twin?"

"Why do I always have to be the good twin?" said Garnet. "Hey, maybe we're changing around. We're starting already. You're crying— and I'm not!"

"You will still be my best friend, won't you? You won't go all ritzy and snooty and look down on me?" I said.

"Don't talk nonsense," said Garnet.

"And you will write to me?"

"Every single day. And you write to me too."

"I promise."

"You don't always keep your promises."

"But this is a promise I'll keep, I swear. And I also promise that I'll never ever be mean to you again, Garnet."

"You'd better not swear on *that* promise," said Garnet, laughing.

But she cried a little when she and Dad went off in the car. We *all* cried.

Garnet's taken the accounts book with her. She's going to write in it every day and then show it to me when she comes home. I've nearly finished this memorandum book already.

I'll have to get another. Bigger, so I can write more. I'll look and see if there's an office supply store in Hineford on Saturday. Rose is going to drive me there. She's found out about this Saturday drama club. So I'm joining it.

I was tickled pink when she told me about it. "Thanks, Rose," I said.

Well. It was more of a mumble. But she heard.

"It's okay, Ruby. I'm dying to go to Hineford to see some decent stores. I'll have a lovely time in the shopping center while you do your drama session and then we'll meet and have lunch. Yes?"

"You bet," I said.

She's not quite so bad as I thought, Rose.

It's time I started some serious drama training. For my big moment when the television people get in touch and ask me to audition. Because they still *might*. If this twitty Twins at St. Clare's series is a success they might want to do another Enid Blyton book. One of the Famous Five stories, maybe. The leading part is this fierce tomboy girl, Georgina. I could play her easy as pie. I've even got the right haircut now.

When Dad gives me a big hug, he ruffles all the bristles and calls me his little Scrubbing Brush. Dad's needed quite a lot of hugs. Because he's missing Garnet so much.

We're all missing her.

I'm missing her most.

But she's all right. She sort of likes it.

I'll stick her first letter on this page.

Dearest Ruby,

I'm here! At Marnock Heights: I feel just like one of the girls in these old school books. I cried a bit after Dad left but this lovely big girl put her arm around me. She's called Jamilla and she's my sheepdog. That doesn't mean she barks at me, she just shows me where everything is, the classrooms and my bedroom and the dining room. We had chicken and fries for supper. And Jamilla gave me half a Kit Kat.

I'm in the bedroom now and there are three other girls and we're all setting our alarms for midnight so we can have our first feast! The girl in the bed next to me is called Lucy, and she wears little glasses and she's got a toy rabbit to take to bed and a real rabbit in the zoo and she says I can share it if I want. She wants to be my best friend and I said yes but you're my bestest best friend, Ruby. With lots and lots of love from Garnetxxxxx

P.S. I miss you so.

Oh, Garnet. I miss you too. Ever so ever so much.

But we're still Ruby and Garnet, even though you're there and I'm here.

We're going to be Ruby and Garnet forever.